MURDER IN FULBRIDGE VILLAGE

HENRY FLEMING INVESTIGATES

BOOK ONE

JAY GILL

VISIT WWW.JAYGILL.NET

～

Visit my website for new releases and special offers: www.jaygill.net

WELCOME NOTE

Welcome, readers old and new. I'm excited to share with you the first *Henry Fleming Investigates* mystery, which was forced to wait backstage whilst other writing was completed, but has finally reached the page for you all to enjoy.

These mysteries are set in 1920s England and form part of a series although, of course, each case can be read as a standalone. In addition, within the pages you will find no graphic violence, bedroom shenanigans or strong language.

These stories are spoiler-free and, in the best tradition of the whodunnit, the cast of suspects, along with a smattering of red-herrings, will have you guessing until the very end, when our great detective presides over his *grand reveal*.

And so, without further ado, let's discover the truth behind what took place in the village of Fulbridge.

Fulbridge Village 1923

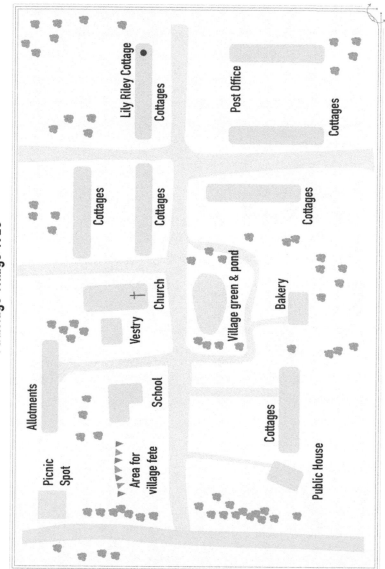

Cast List

Henry Fleming (Private detective)

Skip (Fleming's four-legged friend. Yellow Labrador)

Mrs Clayton (Fleming's housekeeper)

Lewis (Fleming's gardener)

Lily Riley (Famed author, retired) and Kitty (Much loved cat)

William Riley (Lily's late husband)

Jonathan Ardern (Vicar)

Barbara Ardern (Vicar's wife)

Valerie Toussaint

Olivia Bennett

Keith Bennett

Warren Silvers (Artist)

Petunia Longbottom

Dicky (Richard) Longbottom

Inspector Carp

Arthur Pudding (Olivia Bennett's friend)

An Extract from the Diary of
H. K. Fleming, Esq.

Fulbridge Village, 1923

I'm pleased to be visiting my good friend, Lily Riley. She has made me most welcome, and already I can feel my spirits lifting.

What a tranquil and picturesque village Fulbridge is. With its thatched cottages, cobbled streets, village green and historic church, it is the very epitome of Englishness. I have visited many corners of the world and can say with complete honesty that, on a warm and quiet summer's afternoon, there are few places on earth I would rather be than an English village.

Lily has thrown herself, with gusto, into the making of jams and preserves. It would appear I am to become something of a guinea pig as she plans for me to sample some of her most popular recipes, as well as some new formulations! It's an undertaking I shall relish (no pun intended). My sweet tooth was made for such a task!

∽

Today we attended the Fulbridge village fete. Lily showed her strawberry jam and spicy tomato chutney, which won gold and silver respectively! There was a dog show, so it's a shame Skip's not with me. I'm sure my four-legged friend's tail would have been set wagging by all the different shapes, sizes and breeds taking part.

~

My stay here in Fulbridge has taken a dramatic turn for the worse and I'm concerned for Lily. She's taken to her room and is in a great deal of distress after the murder of a close friend.

Having met Inspector Carp, the lead detective, I'm left with mixed feelings about the man. I can only hope he is more capable than first impressions would have me believe. His inexperience and assumptions leave me astounded and itching to intervene.

The inspector has made it quite clear to me, however, that I am to leave the investigation in the hands of the police and, hard as that may be, unless the need arises, or my expertise is requested, that is precisely what I shall do.

CHAPTER ONE

DORSET, ENGLAND, 1923

In the sunny walled rose garden of Avonbrook Cottage, in Shinton Moor, on the south coast of England, Henry Fleming's dark brown eyes appraised the scene. Dressed somewhat inappropriately for the task in Savile Row suit trousers and waistcoat, he poked at a green clump with his garden fork. He felt certain it was broad-leaved dock. He stuck the fork into the ground beside it and, allowing the fork to do the work, teased it out while attempting to remove as much root as possible.

He shook his head disappointedly, and ran a hand through his receding hairline. He'd been toiling away all morning in the baking sun and made little progress.

'I should have left it to Lewis,' he grumbled. 'What was I thinking?'

Skip, Fleming's yellow Labrador, raised his head and gave a puzzled look. He'd been sleeping in the sun, but had woken to the sound of his master's grumblings.

'I'm making a mess of things, Skip. I'll have to swallow my pride and ask Lewis to take over.'

The job of weeding and dressing the garden borders should have been started weeks ago when the soil was soft but he'd insisted he'd like to do the work himself, and so it had been left.

'With a dry spring and early summer, the earth has baked harder than the rocks of Vesuvius,' he complained.

Skip whimpered sympathetically then laid his head back down and closed his eyes.

After ten more minutes, Henry took the pocket watch from his waistcoat and checked the time. He cast his eyes over the border once more, and sighed inwardly. He was disappointed at how little impact the morning's toil had made. As much as he loved his roses, and the idea of working the garden, he was ready to call it a day.

Skip opened an eye.

'Reluctantly, I'll have to admit defeat, my friend. Too many of Mrs Clayton's sweet treats have taken their toll.' He chuckled and patted his waistline. As a gentleman of average height and build, he'd noted a bit more tummy of late, which he put down to his incurable sweet tooth.

Skip struggled to his paws and yawned.

'I'll apologise and turn this over to the expert. Lewis will understand. It's apparent that despite best efforts, my talents lie in work that's less physical in nature. I should have listened to my own advice. As I've told you many times, my four-legged friend, a person should work to their strengths wherever possible.'

Skip listened intently, wagging his tail as Fleming stroked and patted his hot, yellow coat.

'Let's do what I've been promising for far too long. I'll write to Lily Riley.'

Lily had invited him to visit her some weeks ago, but it hadn't been possible due to a prior engagement in the Netherlands. 'It's time for a change of scenery, Skip. Something completely different. Away from the daily routine of Avonbrook Cottage.'

Skip let out a bark.

'Sorry, old friend, you won't be coming with me this time. Mrs Clayton will look after you.'

Skip's whole body wagged at the mention of Fleming's housekeeper. Mrs Clayton and Skip had a special bond cemented by kitchen titbits and long walks.

'Come on, old chap. Let's find her. If I remain at Avonbrook much longer, attending to the never-ending list of chores I've foolishly set myself, I might lose my mind completely.' He smiled at Skip and gave him a wink. 'I've no doubt the rose garden will be completed while I visit my friend.' He threw a stick for Skip. 'You know something, old boy. I'm suddenly filled with immense cheer.'

~

LILY RILEY SAT on the bench in her front garden, reading a book on Egyptian mythology. From there, she could enjoy the sunshine, listen to the birds and watch the back and forth on Fulbridge High Street. Not that there was much to observe today. With her maid on holiday she was alone. Besides the postman, and the baker's delivery lad, she had only spoken to two other people. Both were neighbours.

Keith Bennett had little to say and was in a hurry. He'd waved and agreed the weather was delightful.

Valerie Toussaint had stopped and sat with her for a while. Unfortunately, she had wanted only to discuss their business venture. Not only did Valerie possess a natural beauty that even in her advancing years could stop men in their tracks, but she'd been gifted brains as well. A combination that, for some reason, hadn't been enough for Valerie's ex-husband.

'The money's on its way,' Valerie had said. 'Our investors at Whittingworth Foods are drawing up the paperwork. They told me once again how much they love the traditional English taste and brand and want more. I was thinking that besides the jam, we could send samples of our chutney and marmalade, perhaps some of that delicious relish, too.'

'I'll prepare more, although I'm a little long in the tooth for all this. I don't have the energy I used to.'

'The money'll change all that. You'll soon be living in luxury, drinking champagne for breakfast brought to you by your butler. We could visit the pyramids together. Take a boat up the Nile. Even fund our very own archaeological dig!'

'I must say, that does sound appealing, but a lot of hard work. I'm quite content here in the village. Teaching at the school a few hours a week, reading and just pottering keeps me happy.'

Valerie patted her friend's hand. 'We'll see.'

All her life Lily had done her utmost to avoid risk. Fortunately, her parents had been wealthy, so she'd been well educated and had been taught caution regarding financial matters. It was in her late thirties, and still unmarried, that her fiction writing, which was published using a male pseudonym, brought success, but also intense curiosity as to the author's identity. Fortunately, when she was eventually unmasked it didn't affect her popularity. Her identity as a woman may have initially surprised her readers, but had no effect on sales, and with each new novel her popularity increased.

Lily had married late. William had been a kind and gentle soul whom she'd met while holidaying in Scotland. Their paths had crossed whilst visiting Loch Ness and they'd found themselves chatting. He'd had no idea she was famous and Lily thought his down-to-earth manner both refreshing and attractive. She learned he was a clerk at a brick-makers'. They eventually married which, in a bid to keep it from the newspapers, they did in a small private church.

He'd been a reliable man, and it was William who'd kept her feet on the ground when her celebrity threatened to encroach on their modest lifestyle. They'd made a good team and enjoyed life together until the end. His illness had been mercifully short, though it was at this time that her writing lost its appeal and she decided to step back from that aspect of her life.

Lily wondered what he would have made of her imminent fortune. When the offer had come in to buy her brand of jams, Lily had managed to bat away Valerie's persistence with a smile and a dismissive wave of a hand. However, it was a lot of money Whittingworth Foods were offering, and Valerie seemed sure it was a genuine, once in a lifetime offer. The investors appeared to adore the taste, and Lily's celebrity, fading as it was, still had appeal. Having her late fame associated with the product concerned her. She'd worked hard to leave that life behind and, in truth, the whole situation made her feel uncomfortable. Her name would be on jars all over London. Harrods and Fortnum and Mason had already agreed to stock her jams and, with Whittingworth Foods' connections with retailers in the United States, the market potential was enormous. Yet, her biggest concern was that, if she refused, her decision would jeopardise her friendship with Valerie. She had therefore decided that Valerie should also benefit from the sale. Having been left almost penniless through no fault of her own when her scoundrel husband had left, it seemed this opportunity would give Valerie a second chance.

Lily looked up. The postman stopped and handed her a letter. She examined it and knew immediately from the quality of the paper and familiar handwriting, it was from Henry Fleming.

She opened it eagerly. He wanted to visit and stay in the village for a few days. Lily jumped to her feet and rushed inside. She needed to reply immediately. There was also work to be done – the cottage was a mess. Then she remembered with frustration that

Penny, her maid, was on holiday at the seaside. She wondered if she should put Henry off, but she'd waited such a long time for him to visit again she decided, there and then, that he'd have to take her as she was.

~

'GOOD MORNING, VALERIE.' Keith Bennett's gentle features and large, soft eyes appeared from behind the front wall of his garden. Smiling warmly, he got to his feet and brushed the dirt from his trousers.

Valerie giggled, which served only to make her seem more beautiful. 'I didn't see you there. You made me jump. Were you hiding?'

As her red hair dazzled in the morning sun, Keith stuttered and tried to find words. He attempted to remember what he'd been wanting to say, but found his mind had gone blank. 'Of course not. I'm sorry.' His face flushed red. 'I was staking the delphiniums.' He held up a ball of string and a wooden cane.

'I was teasing. I guessed that's what you were doing. They're stunning again this year. Tall and elegant. You're so clever. I adore them.'

'I know you do.' He smoothed his greying hair. 'Have you seen this plant? It's a new variety to me. I sowed in early spring and it's doing really well.' He pointed to a clump of pinky-orange flowers beside the front gate.

'That's very pretty.'

'Guess what it's called?'

She shook her head and smiled broadly. 'I've no idea.'

'The plant's a columbine, or granny's bonnet as some call it, and it's named... Lady Valerie!'

'Well I never. My namesake.'

'I thought it would tickle you. I know how much you enjoy the garden.'

'I hope you'll save me some seeds and I'll do my best to grow it in my own garden. I wish I had your green fingers. I really don't know how you do it. You've created your very own small piece of Eden right here in Fulbridge.'

Keith's nose wrinkled with delight. 'It's not that difficult. Nature does most of the hard work.'

She held up some envelopes. 'I'd better be off or I'll miss today's collection. Don't forget to save me some Lady Valerie.'

'I won't. I'll bring it on in the greenhouse for you.' Keith went back to staking his plants, watching out of the corner of his eye as Valerie continued up the cobbled high street to the post office. It wasn't until she was almost out of sight that he realised she'd dropped one of her envelopes.

In the top left corner Valerie had written 'Confidential'. It was addressed to Whittingworth Foods.

He flapped the envelope up and down as he wondered what to do. He decided that if he moved quickly, he might catch her at the postbox. He darted to the house and called to Olivia.

'I'm just popping out, Livvy. I won't be long.'

'What's that?' Olivia called back.

He could hear from her raised voice she was in the kitchen at the other end of the cottage.

'I said, I'm nipping out for a bit.'

'Where're you going?'

He hesitated. 'The vicar mentioned a bouquet for church on Sunday. I thought I'd ask if there's anything he'd like me to include.' He suddenly felt very guilty using the vicar, of all people, as his excuse to pursue Valerie.

'Really, Keith? Do you have to?'

'It won't take long. Look, I've got to go.'

'You haven't forgotten I want you to come with me to town to find a new blouse?'

He groaned inwardly. He'd hoped she'd changed her mind about clothes shopping. 'We can go as soon as I return.' He closed the front door before she could say any more and quick-marched up the high street.

~

OLIVIA BENNETT HAD JUST FINISHED SANDWICHING two perfectly golden sponges together with strawberry jam and cream, singing softly to herself as she sieved a fine dusting of icing sugar over the top, when she had heard voices coming from the front garden of the cottage. She moved to the window and peered out. Keith was chatting with someone. She was unable to make out who it was but, from his animated movements, she instinctively knew.

Valerie Toussaint, whose husband had run off to who knows where, with who knows who and was now no doubt looking for husband number two.

Olivia had watched as Keith leaned over and pointed at one of his plants, the pair of them laughing together. Olivia felt the need to join them, but was glued to the spot, stunned by Keith's behaviour. *What on earth was he thinking?* She had wanted so badly to hear what they were saying.

A few moments later, Valerie made her excuses and continued on her way. Olivia had noticed how Keith pretended not to be watching her departure. He opened the front gate and went out onto the pavement; picked something up. An envelope. Valerie must have dropped it.

The front door opened.

'I'm just popping out, Livvy. I won't be long,' he'd called.

'What's that?' Olivia had yelled back. She knew exactly what he'd said and where he was going *and* that he'd lie about it.

The front door closed.

Olivia now stood staring at the beautiful Victoria sponge. She thumped it with her fist, picked up the squashy mess and hurled it with all her might through the open back door onto the vegetable garden.

~

Petunia Longbottom squinted at a fine ring in the glass cabinet. 'What do you think of this, Dicky?'

Her husband, Richard, put down the marble mantel clock he'd been admiring, which he believed to be French, mid to late nineteenth century.

'Costume jewellery at best,' he said without hesitation. He rubbed his dark beard thoughtfully. Towering over his petite wife, he added, 'It's over-priced, that's for sure. The owner's obviously trying to hoodwink an amateur.'

Petunia tilted her head to get a better look. 'Do you think so?'

'No doubt whatsoever. It's how these out of the way antique shops survive.'

'It's very pretty.' She tucked her shoulder length dark wavy hair behind her ear.

'If you like it, I'm sure the owner will be happy to negotiate but I'm certainly not paying the asking price.'

'Please don't make a scene. I want to have a nice, calm day. No drama.'

He raised an eyebrow. 'Drama? I don't know what you mean.'

Petunia nudged her husband playfully.

Dicky's fingers drummed against the glass cabinet. 'I want you to try it on. Where is the man?' He picked up a little brass bell that sat on the cashier's desk and tinkled it several times.

'Never mind, let's forget it,' Petunia said. 'We can come back another time.'

Dicky cursed and rang the bell again. 'Hold on. Here he comes.'

An elderly bespectacled man in a tatty brown cardigan appeared from the back of the shop. 'I'm sorry. I was on the telephone. My wife's not well, so I'm on my own this week.'

Petunia smiled sympathetically.

'How can I help you today?'

Dicky's eyes narrowed as he tried to size up the old man. 'The piece here.' He pointed at the ring. 'It seems a little expensive, don't you think?'

Petunia sighed at Dicky's bluntness. 'We're curious to see if there's any flexibility on price, is what he's trying to say.'

The dealer opened the cabinet. 'Let's take a look.'

'It's very pretty,' Petunia said as he placed the ring on a black velvet cloth.

'My wife's taken a shine to it, although I'm certain it's nothing but costume jewellery. But you know how women can be when they set their mind on something.'

Petunia glared at Dicky. 'Enough of that talk or you'll be sleeping in the shed at the end of the garden tonight.'

Dicky adjusted his collar. 'Sorry, sweetheart.'

The dealer encouraged Petunia to try the ring on for size. 'You have a fine eye. See how the jewels sparkle? It really suits your elegant hand.'

Petunia nodded and grinned from ear to ear. 'I love it.'

Dicky returned to the subject of the price tag. 'The thing is, there's no way that red stone's a ruby.'

'You're correct, sir. It's an Almandine garnet and diamond cluster. Exquisite, isn't it? With a ring like this, it's the quality of the diamonds that sets the price.' The dealer checked the tag and tutted. 'Oh dear.'

'What's wrong?' Petunia asked.

'Well, you see, this is a new piece and with my wife suddenly being taken ill, I allowed my daughter to put out some new stock, including this particular ring. She's got the price tags mixed up. It's worth considerably more than this, so I'll have to remove it from sale. I do apologise.' He put out his hand for the ring's return.

Petunia's face dropped. She looked up at Dicky. 'We'll find something else.'

Dicky straightened his blazer. 'It's a gift for my wife's birthday.'

'I'm sorry,' the dealer said, and began taking the new stock from the cabinet. 'I need to check the prices of all these myself. I love my daughter dearly but ask her to do the simplest task and – well – this is the result.'

'It doesn't matter,' Petunia said. 'We'll keep looking. That dress we saw will be perfect.'

Dicky lowered his voice. 'How much for the ring?'

The dealer shook his head.

'How much?'

The dealer considered the question. 'Diamonds like these...?' He held the ring up to the light, so it sparkled and flashed. 'I'd need to add at least fifty per cent.'

Dicky swallowed hard.

Petunia put a hand on his arm. 'It doesn't matter. Let's go.'

'Twenty per cent,' Dicky insisted.

'Forty-five,' the dealer countered.

'Twenty-five.'

The dealer shook his head. 'As it's your wife's birthday gift...' he smiled warmly at Petunia, 'and I know my dear wife would want me to do what I can, she has a heart of pure gold, I'll accept just thirty per cent more than the price marked on the tag. It's really all I can do.'

Dicky shot out a hand. 'Deal.'

Petunia jumped with delight.

As they left the shop, it suddenly dawned on Dicky what the sly old fox had done and how completely he'd been suckered. He clenched his jaw and swallowed his pride. 'Are you happy, birthday girl?'

Petunia squeezed her husband's arm and held out her hand to show off the ring. 'Ecstatic!'

CHAPTER TWO

The thatched cottage was modest, comfortable and after some frantic tidying, clutter free. Apart from, that is, a large collection of ornaments, mainly Egyptian, and lots and lots of historical books. There were sash windows and low ceilings with wooden beams. Currently, the whole place was filled with the heady perfume of jam that Lily had been making in large batches.

Lily Riley and Fleming were sitting at a small table beside a large window in her kitchen. She was a thin, active, elderly lady, her greying hair fixed in a bun atop her head, whose eyes still shone with youth.

Having offered him a fruit scone, Lily opened a jar of her prize-winning plum jam, while Fleming poured the steaming tea.

Though he hadn't yet seen it, Fleming noted

evidence of a cat. Two small empty blue and white china saucers sat by the back door, and there was fur on the armchair beside the fireplace.

Lily added a healthy dollop of clotted cream to her scone. 'I love this room. On summer days like this, the sun pours in. Better still is the view down the garden. First thing in the morning I like to feed the birds that visit. I sprinkle a few crumbs and scatter seeds on the window ledge. It might sound silly, but I sometimes give them names.'

'It doesn't sound silly at all,' Fleming said. 'Do you ever get lonely here by yourself?'

'Never. I teach at the school a few hours a week. I also have a lovely group of friends. Hopefully, you'll get to meet one or two of them. We usually see each other most days. I also have Kitty, my cat, who keeps me company. In the evenings I read or listen to the radio. I'm not sure where Kitty's got to. I think maybe having a new face around has shocked her. She's a sensitive little thing. I love her dearly.' Lily sipped her tea. 'Henry, if you don't mind my saying, I've often wondered if perhaps you don't think it's time to move on; find someone to share your life with after... well, after what happened?'

Fleming stiffened slightly and sat a little straighter.

'Oh my goodness! I'm so sorry, Henry. What on earth was I thinking?' Lily cried. 'I didn't mean to pry.'

'It's all right, Lily.' Henry smiled gently. 'I'm quite content. My work keeps me busy. In whatever spare time I have, I take long walks with Skip, and enjoy my books. I'm currently reading some Dickens. I try to read something of his work at least once a year. There's always something new to learn from them.'

The pair nodded their heads.

'Do you miss the writing?' Fleming asked. 'I've read little that matched your heroine's sharp social criticism and humour.'

'That was so long ago now. I feel sure you're being polite.'

'On the contrary. You know better than anyone, I never lie.' His eyes shone.

'It's a fault of yours. That's true.'

The pair chuckled.

'Before you refuse and make your excuses, I want you to know that I won't hear of you staying at a hotel. I mentioned in my letter that I'd make up the spare room, and I have.'

'Tongues will wag.'

'Let them. I don't care a fig what others say. I'm far too thick-skinned to worry about all that stuff and nonsense.'

'I've a feeling there's no use in my protesting.'

'None at all. You're welcome to stay as long as

you'd like. I've put fresh towels on the chair beside the bed.'

'You're a generous friend,' Fleming said.

'Nonsense! It's been far too long since we spent any proper time together. I'd like to catch up and learn about your exploits. I read with excitement that you were in the Netherlands recently. Can I assume you played a part in solving the theft of young Princess Juliana's tiara?'

'I couldn't possibly say,' said Fleming with a twinkle in his eye.

'Congratulations. I'm sure the royal family were exceedingly grateful.' She put the lid back on the plum jam. 'What did you think of my jam?'

'Delicious.' Having earlier taken note of all the jars on shelves in the kitchen, he said, 'You're quite the cottage industry.'

'An award-winning cottage industry,' Lily added modestly. 'These days I only enter the village fete to support the parish. I've little interest in winning. That said, I have a fine strawberry jam that's going to knock the judges' socks off.'

'You sound confident?'

'I enjoy the fact the parish comes together and money's raised for good causes,' Lily chuckled.

'It sounds like a lot of fun.'

'You'd be surprised at how competitive the Fulbridge village fete can be.'

'Is there prize money?'

'Well, nothing to write home about. Being able to label the jam as prize-winning can boost sales. Winners receive a rosette and a modest cash prize. It's more about the pride of winning. However, on occasion, sadly, some competitors forget it's just a bit of fun.'

'In what way?' Fleming asked.

'Last year, I read about a man called Paul Trout in Cornwall who was caught stealing villager Charlie Elton's carrots. Carrots destined for their own village show, I might add. He was spotted visiting the allotment in the dead of night and pulling them out of the ground.'

'That's criminal.'

'I wouldn't have believed someone would go to such ridiculous lengths to beat a fellow competitor, but Charlie Elton caught him in the act. He'd stayed hidden on his plot all night, along with the local police constable.'

'The police were involved?'

'Yes. It even made the local paper, would you believe? A friend sent me a copy. Not only that, but the year before *Elton* had claimed his biggest ever pumpkin, certain to achieve gold and break the village record, was stamped on as it grew on his allotment. At the time, he pointed a finger at Trout but there was no proof; Trout countering that the pumpkin had simply collapsed under its own weight, a natural phenomenon due to poor husbandry. Elton was outraged by this slur on his reputation, and pointed out there was a footprint on the pumpkin that proved sabotage.'

There was no hint of a smile on Fleming's face. Only concern. 'It never ceases to amaze me how quickly things can get out of hand when pride and ambition are at stake.'

'Human nature is a curious thing,' Lily agreed. Attempting to lighten the mood, she grinned and added, 'Thankfully, the jams, jellies and preserves competitors are generally a more genial group.'

There was a knock at the back door and Lily introduced her friend Valerie Toussaint. Her startling red hair was tied up in a pale green and blue scarf. She was dressed in a flowery blouse and loose trousers. 'Knock, knock. Just checking you're all set to be beaten this year by the most perfect jam you ever tasted.'

Fleming got to his feet and straightened his waistcoat.

'I'm sorry, Lily, I didn't realise you had company.' Valerie's striking blue eyes met Fleming's. 'A handsome gentleman, too. You sly old bird. Keeping him all to yourself?'

'This is my good friend, Henry Fleming,' Lily

corrected. She disliked such talk. 'He's visiting for a few days. He's the private detective I mentioned.'

'The celebrated Henry Fleming? It's a delight to meet you. Are you here to solve a case? Has there been a kidnapping, or murder, or have thieves taken the lead from the church roof again?'

'Nothing so dramatic. Fortunately, I'm simply visiting my good friend. A little holiday to recharge the body and rest the mind.'

'Will Mrs Fleming be joining you?'

Fleming was about to say there was no Mrs Fleming, when Lily intervened. 'Yes. We're hoping she'll join us very soon.' She glanced at the kitchen clock. 'Any minute now, in fact.'

Valerie smiled mischievously. 'In that case, I look forward to seeing you both at the fete tomorrow. You will be coming, I presume?'

Lily and Valerie both looked at Fleming.

He nodded like a cornered child. 'I wouldn't miss it for the world.'

'Wonderful! I must be off. I'm doing the rounds and rallying the troops. This year promises to be the best turnout ever.' Valerie retreated, and Lily breathed a sigh of relief.

'You can thank me later,' Lily chuckled. 'I love her dearly, I do. However, it's clear she's on the hunt for a new husband. If she learned you were unmarried, she'd be all over you like a rash.'

'You needn't worry about me. I consider myself married.'

Lily felt a pang of sadness for Fleming. 'How about I wash these plates and we go for a walk? I need to get some bread for the morning and we can explore the village a little.'

'I'll do the dishes.'

'Nonsense. Talk like that will see you thrown out on your ear.'

Fleming smiled. 'I'll fetch my case and take it to my room.'

Kitty decided to make an appearance. Like a ballerina, she tip-toed along the dry stone wall separating the garden from the next cottage. She hopped down and came in through the open door. Sitting in the pantry doorway, she studied Fleming as he passed by and headed upstairs with his suitcase.

CHAPTER THREE

Fulbridge village has a small church, an adjacent vicarage, a village green with a pond and ducks at its centre. The green itself is too small to hold the village fete, and so it is held each year on the school playing field.

Fleming understood completely why Lily who, at the height of her celebrity, had withdrawn from the limelight, would want to retire and live her life in this tranquil corner of the world away from all the press interest. To some, it made no sense at all. Why would she give it all up and withdraw from the adoration? Yet Fleming, having met celebrities the world over, understood all too well how fame can be a double-edged sword. The pressure and expectation that comes with forever being in the limelight can take its toll. And so, with the warmth of the sun on his back, the sound of birdsong in his ear, and the scent of honeysuckle filling his nostrils, her choice made utter sense.

As they passed the village school, Lily pointed. 'That's my classroom. I no longer teach full time but help out a few hours a week.'

The red brick building, playground, and small clock tower reminded him of his own childhood. 'What a pretty building in which to go to school.'

Olivia Bennett was tying bunting to the school's railings and cast iron gates. She wore a white straw hat, a pleated skirt and flowing blouse. Her dark hair had come loose and a thick curl bounced as she energetically organised tasks. Keith, who was sweating profusely, raised a hand in greeting. He chose not to join the conversation and instead continued to hammer small signs into the ground, which pointed to the village pub.

'Olivia's showing her raspberry jam, mango chutney and a chilli sauce,' Lily said.

With a wave of her hand, Olivia instructed Keith to place his next sign further down the road. He obliged without complaint. 'This is the first year there's been a competition for chilli sauce but we have to keep up with the times,' Olivia said over her shoulder as she tied an enormous flag to the school gates.

Lily's eyes lit up. 'It's quite exciting. I'm not a big

fan of spicy sauces myself, but it's going to be terrific fun to watch the judging.'

Fleming listened with interest. 'I don't envy the judges. From experience, I'd be surprised if they can taste anything after sampling the first one or two.'

'Barbara, the vicar's wife, is one of the judges. Apparently, she and Jonathan, the vicar, both love spicy food. The fierier the better. They spent several years in Asia doing missionary work before returning to England,' Olivia explained.

Fleming kept an eye on Keith as he toiled away, knocking in the signs. He looked very pale and was sweating profusely. He lifted his head and smiled Fleming's way before hammering in another post. He then leaned against a wall and wiped his face with a brightly coloured paisley handkerchief.

'I'm feeling so nervous about tomorrow,' Olivia continued. 'Keith keeps telling me to calm down, but I'd kill to win first prize in at least one of the categories. Not literally, of course. I mean, I'd love to win, but not that badly.' She laughed nervously at her poor choice of words and eyed the detective.

'From what I've heard in such a short time, I'm beginning to realise village fetes can be a little cutthroat,' Fleming said.

'Nothing serious enough to concern you,' Lily chuckled. 'It's all very petty.'

Olivia crossed her arms. 'I'm not so sure. You wouldn't believe the underhand tactics that go on.'

Lily shook her head. 'It's a harmless enough pastime. The shows are a wonderful way to share one's creativity.'

Olivia wrinkled her nose. 'She's so modest. Everyone knows your jams are the benchmark. How many times have you won that category now?'

'I don't think it's many. Two or three at most.'

'Don't believe a word of it,' Olivia insisted to Fleming.

She turned to Lily. 'Petunia told me you have a secret jam recipe that's been passed down through your family. She also said you told her you'd take that secret to the grave. To me, that sounds like someone who takes their preserves very seriously indeed.'

Lily forced a smile. 'I don't think you should believe everything you hear. We all know Petunia Longbottom's a serious competitor.'

'And that's being polite.'

'We'll let you get on, Olivia. We need to get to the bakery before it closes.'

Fleming noticed Lily had become quieter as they arrived at the bakery. 'You appear upset.'

'I'm okay. People can be so hurtful. All I've ever done is try to be a supportive member of the community. I'll help anyone who needs it and I've certainly helped Petunia many times. She's a complicated, short-tempered woman who often speaks without thinking of the consequences. Comments like hers make me wonder what she's saying behind my back.'

'Tell me the truth,' Fleming teased. 'Do you have a secret recipe stashed away in a locked box beneath the floorboards under your bed?'

'Of course not. It's in the false wall behind the fireplace,' Lily chuckled. 'I simply put love into what I do. As I'm sure all my fellow competitors also do. I also grow my own fruit rather than using shop-bought, as has become the fashion. Maybe that's the difference that helps me win?' She patted his arm. 'Thank you for attempting to cheer me up. However, these days, sometimes the thought of winning fills me with dread, rather than joy. Do you understand what I mean? I've even considered not entering the show this year.'

A voice made them turn. Warren Silvers carried a wicker basket, inside which an enormous onion rested on a plush golden cushion. 'This, lady and gentleman, is my vegetable entry. Isn't she a beauty?' He beamed with pride. 'I've named her The Duchess of Onionshire. I've always *adored* the Royal Family.' He put out a hand. 'You must be the brilliant detective Henry Fleming, lovely to meet you.' It was apparent news of Fleming's arrival had spread already.

Warren's face became serious. 'You do realise, Mrs

Lily Riley, that without you at the Fulbridge village fete, there really would be no point attending. You're the star of the show. The one to beat. The champion of champions. For many of us, it's all part of the fun. I know all too well how catty some people can be. Look at me.' He ran a hand up and down his red trousers which he'd teamed with a green and mustard striped jacket.

'Warren's an artist. His paintings are quite something.'

He bowed as though greeting the queen. 'I'm not your average village resident. I'm far too flamboyant for some, so I've had my fair share of hurtful remarks. I ignore spiteful people and instead focus on spreading cheer and sunshine.' He took Lily's hand. 'That, my lovely lady, is what you must do.'

'Warren, you're a ray of sunshine, and never forget it.'

'Now, reassure me you intend to enter.'

Lily nodded. 'I was simply letting off steam. I'll be entering.'

'Good. You can expect me to give you a run for your money. My raspberry jam is a marvel. Its depth of colour and consistency better than ever before.'

'I'm so pleased. Good luck.' Warren continued on his way.

Fleming noticed that a short distance on Warren

stopped and showed off his onion to a couple who were also headed towards the bakery.

The shop had very little choice, but they purchased sausage rolls for dinner and a white bloomer for the morning.

The couple Fleming had seen were Jonathan Ardern, the vicar, and his wife, Barbara. They arrived as Lily and Fleming came out.

'It's such a glorious day we thought we'd take a stroll and check what time our order of cupcakes will be ready for collection in the morning,' the vicar explained. His long, narrow, tanned face beamed.

'The cupcakes are for the raffle,' Barbara said. Dressed in white and pastel tones, and wearing flat shoes, she looked like the archetypal modern vicar's wife.

'The cupcakes were Barbara's idea,' the vicar added. 'Traditionally, we've provided a selection of local cheeses, but Barbara suggested cupcakes would be more exciting.'

'It's been cheese for five years now, Jonathan. It's time for a change.' Fleming noticed Barbara hide a trembling hand by placing the other on top.

'I'm certainly not arguing, Barbara,' he added hastily. 'Although I admit I'm not one for innovation, that's for sure.'

Fleming eyed the vicar's shoes, which were filthy.

Polished shoes were something Fleming was a stickler for whenever and wherever possible.

The vicar felt he needed to explain his grubby attire. 'I was tending the vegetable patch this morning and got a little muddy. Unfortunately, the deer have been at my prize rhubarb. Of course, I don't mind sharing my bounty with them, but they might have left me some.' He laughed loudly, causing his wife to shudder.

'We really must be going,' Barbara said. 'Lovely to meet you, Mr Fleming. Good luck tomorrow, Lily.'

CHAPTER FOUR

It was late Saturday morning and the day of the village fete. Lily had left early to prepare her entries and help out where needed. Fleming finished his toast and marmalade and sipped his tea. When Kitty appeared, he made sure she had her breakfast of baked mackerel. He then cleared and washed up the breakfast things. As he did so he reminded himself that the village fete should be enjoyable, and that making an excuse so he might not attend, would be bad form.

Having closed the cottage door securely behind him, he headed down the cobbled high street towards the church. The area had been transformed into a celebration of village life. Yesterday's quiet high street was now noisy and bristling with visitors.

Fleming bought a ticket at the gate. Valerie, who was acting as a steward, pointed him towards a large tent where Lily was waiting. 'I presume Mrs Fleming will be along shortly?' She gave him a wink and a knowing smile.

'I think you know the answer to that,' Fleming replied pleasantly. They both laughed. He decided to make a beeline for the show tent and check on Lily.

He passed the vicar, who had his head and hands pushed through a large board on which was painted a pirate with a parrot on his shoulder. A young girl threw a wet sponge at him. Her brother joined in. The pair appeared to be enjoying it immensely and giggled uncontrollably as the vicar laughed and yelled in protest. 'Unfair! One at a time!'

As Fleming approached the show tent, he met Lily coming the other way. She looked exasperated and out of breath.

'Are you okay?' he asked.

At the sound of his voice Lily jumped. Her mind had been elsewhere. 'You won't believe it!' she exclaimed. 'Petunia Longbottom and Warren Silvers got into an argument. I tried to calm the situation but in the end I simply had to come away.'

'What was it about?' Fleming asked with concern.

'I overheard Petunia complaining that her jar labels had been deliberately smudged. She accused Warren of sabotaging her chances!'

Fleming looked confused.

Lily clarified the rules. 'Labels should be non-decorative, straight and an appropriate size. It's best to place them centrally on the lower half of the jar.'

Fleming appeared to approve. 'The little details are important!'

'It's very serious for Petunia. Her jar labels look awful. For her, it's disastrous.'

'Can she appeal?'

'There's no evidence of foul play. I can't believe Warren had anything to do with it. My instincts suggest Petunia's simply venting her anger and blaming him because he's on the table next to her. It's all desperately sad.'

'What do the judges say?'

'There are three judges: Barbara the vicar's wife, Valerie Toussaint, and the landlord of the village pub. I tried to speak to Valerie, but I was told it's best that I don't get involved.'

'It sounds as though it's out of your hands.'

'I know, but...'

'As much as you'd like to, you can't sort everything out for everybody. We have a few minutes until the judging is complete, so let's find ourselves a cup of tea. It'll steady your nerves.'

Having savoured a piece of apple cake and a refreshing cuppa, the pair made their way back to the tent to see how Lily's jams had fared.

As the tent was crowded, Fleming waited outside. Standing out of the way, he was unnoticed by Petunia and her husband, Dicky.

'I'm not putting up with it any more, Dicky. I'm sick of it,' Petunia ranted.

'I know you're upset. Please calm down, sweetheart.'

'I'm deadly serious. She can go to hell for all I care.'

Dicky attempted to put a sympathetic arm around his wife, which she swept away. 'Let me speak to her,' he said. 'You're getting too worked up.'

'The woman is all smiles to your face and then stabs you in the back when you're off guard. Let's be honest, she's never liked me. I don't know why. For some reason, she took an instant dislike to me as soon as we arrived in this horrible place. I want to sell up and leave. I despise all the village politics and the clique of uptight, stuck up, buttoned up...'

'Let's not be hasty. This was our dream. We can't let one person ruin it. Once she gets to know you better, she'll love you. I know it.'

'You're wrong, and I can't believe you're saying that. I've given her enough chances to be friends. If I stay here much longer, I'll do or say something I'll regret, so I'm telling you now, Dicky, I want to move to a large town or, better still, back to the city. This place is too claustrophobic.'

Lily returned with a smile on her face. 'That wasn't so bad.'

'How did you do?' Fleming asked.

Petunia spun around and saw Fleming and Lily. Realising Fleming must have heard their conversation, she stomped away with Dicky trotting to keep up.

'First prize for my strawberry jam,' Lily said. 'Silver for my sweet and spicy tomato chutney. I lost to a very worthy winner.'

'Congratulations. You can relax now, and enjoy the rest of the day.'

'I can.' Lily sighed with satisfaction.

'What happened to Petunia's entry?' Fleming asked.

'I heard from Valerie that she withdrew from the competition. She tried to stop her, but Petunia insisted that she had standards to uphold.' She put her hand to her mouth and lowered her voice. 'Petunia used some very colourful language and vowed never to enter the show again.'

Warren came running up to them. His clothes today were even brighter than yesterday's. Green and red checked trousers, suede shoes and an orange shirt with matching waistcoat. He was in floods of tears. Fortunately, they were tears of joy. 'I got silver with The Duchess of Onion-shire and wait for it... I won gold with my spicy apple and walnut chutney!'

He hugged Lily but didn't stop to chat, instead he squealed and ran to a group of equally excited friends who were extravagant with their congratulations.

In the main ring, dogs and their owners had gathered for the dog show where a black and white border collie named Flo was herding Indian Runner ducks. Fleming watched but despite his fascination with the proud looking birds, found his eyes wandering to the people gathered. He saw Keith and Valerie talking. Dicky was having an animated conversation with the vicar and Barbara (Petunia was nowhere to be seen). Olivia Bennett was congratulating Warren but appeared to have one eye on Keith.

As the day's events drew to a close at around five p.m. Fleming helped Lily with her things and they walked back up the cobbled hill to the cottage.

Halfway up they bumped into a flustered Olivia Bennett. 'Have you seen Keith?' she panted. 'After we heard my chilli sauce got first prize, I started to feel a little cold and he went to fetch my jacket from the cottage.'

'Unfortunately, I haven't seen him in quite a while,' Fleming admitted.

Lily raised an eyebrow as she recalled where she'd last seen him. 'Last time I saw him, he was talking to Valerie. I saw them both over by the tombola about thirty minutes ago.'

'If we see him, we'll let him know you're looking for him,' Fleming added. He had hoped Lily might be more sensitive, but perhaps she hadn't cottoned on to their evident friendship.

Olivia's mind appeared to be in a spin. With a speedy 'thank you' she headed back towards the church. Fleming noticed she stopped briefly to speak to Petunia, Dicky, and Warren who were standing together. 'It seems Petunia and Warren have settled their differences over the spoiled jar labels.'

Lily tutted. 'Those two are like cat and dog. I can't work them out. He's incredibly patient with her, devoted almost. As far as I can see, he's no reason to be. She's rude to him and yet he stands by her.'

'He may understand her better than most. A shared experience, perhaps? Something in his own life may afford him insight. When someone, such as Petunia, carries so much intense anger, the source is often a heart full of pain and sorrow, or an experience of mistreatment.'

'It's hard to say on this occasion whether you're talking sense or utter nonsense. I suspect she's simply spoilt. First by her parents and latterly by her husband. Dicky dotes on her.'

'I'm glad to see you're still not afraid to speak your mind and put me in my place,' Fleming said with a grin.

'What else are friends for, if not to speak their mind?'

When they reached the cottage, Lily dumped her things on the kitchen table. 'Will you be all right for a while if I head back to the fete? I feel I should help with the clearing up.'

'I can assist,' Fleming offered.

Lily was insistent. 'That's very generous, but you're a guest and on holiday. Would you mind feeding Kitty and making some sandwiches for dinner?'

Sensing Lily wanted some space and time alone, he agreed. After all, she wasn't used to guests living in her home. Never one to shy away from pitching in he said, 'Shall I put the jams away in the pantry?'

'That would be wonderful. I shan't be long.' Without another word, she disappeared back out of the door.

CHAPTER FIVE

Around 8.30 the same evening, Fleming had repeatedly checked his pocket watch and stood on the cottage doorstep. The light outside was waning and Lily hadn't returned. He checked the time once again. He was certain the tidying away would have been completed some time ago and wondered whether Lily had become distracted by conversation or accepted the offer of a drink at the public house. He decided both scenarios seemed unlikely, especially the latter. And certainly not while she had a guest in her home.

He waited several minutes more then, for the second time that day, headed down the cobbled street to the village. It was considerably quieter than it had been earlier and the air felt cool.

As he reached the church, Fleming noticed Lily coming the other way. Instinctively, he picked up pace.

She looked as white as her namesake. 'What on earth's the matter?' Fleming asked. 'You look like you've seen a ghost.'

Her mouth was dry and she could barely utter the words. Eventually, after a little encouragement she managed to string a coherent sentence together. 'Valerie Toussaint is dead.' She stared Fleming in the eye. 'Murdered!'

At first, Fleming thought Lily was making a joke. One in bad taste, to be sure. When she didn't smile, he raced into the church. Almost sprinting up the aisle he reached the steps in front of the altar. She lay on her back. Her chest bloody. It was clear Valerie Toussaint had been stabbed through the heart.

Fleming looked about for a murder weapon but found nothing. He then carefully examined the crime scene. Crouching down, he immediately noticed that Valerie clasped a yellow rose petal in her hand. Another yellow petal was on the floor at the end of the aisle. Though there were flowers in the church, he saw no yellow roses.

Realising the inner door was open, he rushed into the vestry in case the murderer had hidden themselves, or the murder weapon, in the small room. It was empty. The vestry had a door to the outside, which was bolted at the top and bottom. The mortice lock too was secured, and no key was evident. Fleming returned to the main church. He moved to the altar and looked back towards the pews and church doors. His trained eye took in everything and everyone.

Keith Bennett appeared. Followed by Petunia and Dicky.

'Please stay back from the crime scene,' Fleming instructed. 'Would someone please alert the police? There has been a murder.'

Warren slumped into a pew and looked like he might faint. Fleming noticed the vicar had now sat Lily down and was comforting her.

As Fleming turned to the altar again, a fine black thread on the tiled floor caught his attention. He knelt down and examined it. With two fingers, he tugged at the thread, which was snagged. With care he teased it away from the tiles.

Fleming moved everyone outside and secured the church. An hour or so later, the police arrived and began taking statements. A gruff voice snapped Fleming out of his thoughts. 'Inspector Fleming?'

'Retired,' Fleming corrected. 'On occasion, I'm a private detective, currently holidaying.'

'I know precisely who you are, Mr Fleming. It's an honour to meet you, sir.'

Fleming shook hands with the young detective. 'Have we met? I seldom forget a face.'

'Not officially. I'm Inspector Carp. I've been sent

from Scotland Yard. I was in the neighbourhood. Mrs Carp and I were visiting friends a few miles away when I got the call from Scotland Yard about this little drama.' He shifted several times from one foot to another. 'You know, it's easy to think it's going to be quieter out here in the sticks. English towns and villages are meant to be places of tranquillity. Of course, you get crime, but when I was a young constable I naively imagined it would be nothing but stolen farm machinery, feuding locals, and burgled country homes.' He shrugged and laughed nervously. 'I've heard a lot about you. You're something of a legend back at the Yard.'

'That's very kind. I proffer advice where I can.'

'I've heard you're a plain talker. I like that. No beating about the bush.'

Fleming smiled politely.

Carp stepped closer. 'Word has it, you're a wily old fox who's a stickler for the law. Solved every case you ever had. Is that true?'

'Almost. But you shouldn't believe everything you hear, Inspector. The truth is often twisted and stories of success exaggerated.'

Carp turned his attention to the matter of the body. 'Nasty business. Murder for sure. No sign of the weapon, though. I guess the killer took it with them.'

'Have the interviews revealed anything of interest?'

'Nothing yet. It's very likely the husband did it. A crime of passion, perhaps?'

Fleming's eyes sparkled, his top lip twitching at Carp's assumptions. 'You'll find the deceased is no longer married and her ex-husband emptied their bank account before departing. He resides abroad with his new bride. You'll check, I'm sure, but I doubt he risked returning all this way to stab his ex-wife in a small parish church.'

'I'll definitely be following that up.' Carp smoothed his moustache. 'I don't suppose you know his name?'

Fleming sighed inwardly and shook his head. 'Out of interest, how many murder cases have you worked, Inspector?'

'Including this one?'

'Yes.'

'Half a dozen.'

'You solved six murder cases?'

'Actually, I worked four cases. I don't know why I exaggerated. Three I solved. The most recent one was taken over by another detective when the trail went cold.' He tugged his collar. 'I was reassigned to a new case. An important one. Very important, in fact. My abilities were never in question. Despite any rumours to the contrary.'

'I see,' said Fleming. He stroked the pocket watch

tucked into his waistcoat. He began to pace while Carp followed.

Carp cleared his throat and puffed out his chest. 'This will be a piece of cake. We have a limited number of suspects. A narrow window of opportunity.'

'Quite so.'

'We're taking statements and the scene is being examined. There'll be a search for the weapon, of course. It's a small community, someone will have very likely seen something. In a sleepy village like this, I doubt we're looking for another Jack the Ripper.'

'What if the act itself was spontaneous? To stab someone through the heart might suggest an act of passion, perhaps?'

'Do you have a theory?'

'It's far too early to say.'

Carp smiled. 'Those brain cells of yours must be working overtime.' He put an unwelcome hand on Fleming's shoulder.

Fleming stopped pacing. 'I can't deny I'm more than a little curious,' he admitted.

'I understand how much you'd like to be involved, sir. Especially with this happening on your doorstep, so to speak, but respectfully, I have to ask that you leave it to the police. I can assure you, we have both the resources and the expertise, we'll have this case wrapped up in no time.'

'I hope you're right, Inspector. This killer should be found as a matter of urgency.'

Fleming wished Carp luck and went to find Lily. He helped her to her feet and, aiding her with his arm, they headed home.

Back at the cottage, Lily was very quiet; dazed by the shock Fleming suspected. He poured her a brandy and her hand trembled as she drank. When she retired to bed, Fleming made himself a pot of strong tea and sat at the small kitchen table, considering what he knew. He took the thread he'd retrieved from his pocket and examined it. He wondered what it meant. Perhaps, it was nothing. Then again, it could be the key to unravelling the whole mystery.

~

LILY DIDN'T RISE for breakfast. Despite his best efforts, Fleming couldn't persuade her to eat any lunch, either. It wasn't until the evening that she dressed for dinner and joined him at the kitchen table, where she managed a few mouthfuls of tomato soup. 'I simply cannot believe Valerie's gone, Henry. She was always so vibrant. I'll miss her awfully.'

Fleming took Lily's ice-cold hand. Her eyes brimmed with tears. Overnight, she appeared to have aged ten years. 'They'll catch the person responsible. It's only a matter of time.'

'The question I keep asking myself over and over is why would somebody do something so vile?'

Fleming had been giving the same question considerable thought. He said nothing, but continued to hold her hand.

'What if the person responsible is a lunatic and attacks someone else?' She shifted her seat closer to him. 'Are all the doors and windows locked?'

'That sort of talk will do you no good at all. You'll end up a prisoner in your own home.'

She looked petrified.

'For your peace of mind,' he conceded, 'I'll check doors and windows before we retire...'

There was a knock at the front door.

Lily almost shrieked. 'Who could that be?'

Fleming opened the door to Inspector Carp.

'I'm sorry to visit so late in the evening,' Carp said. 'As I suspected, this case has progressed at speed.' He smoothed his moustache and proudly raised an eyebrow.

'It's perfectly fine. You're welcome here any time. Won't you come in?'

Carp looked around. His tired eyes scanned the room, eventually settling on Lily. 'I have a few questions for Mrs Riley.'

'What is it?' Lily said.

Fleming offered Carp a seat. 'Why don't you join us? Tea?'

Carp cleared his throat and refused a seat. 'Actually, there isn't time. I want Mrs Riley to accompany me to the station.'

Fleming instinctively stepped between Lily and Carp.

'What does he mean, Henry?' Lily asked. 'Is he arresting me?'

'What's going on, Inspector?' Fleming asked crossly.

'I didn't do anything,' Lily insisted. 'Does he suspect me?'

Carp frowned. 'Don't make this more difficult than it already is, Fleming. We have a witness who saw Lily and Valerie arguing before the murder and she's the last person known to have seen Valerie alive. Then there's the murder weapon. I have it on good authority the weapon used was a type of dagger.'

'What about it?' Fleming asked.

'It's my belief that the murder weapon belongs to Lily?'

'Don't talk nonsense,' Fleming said. He looked at Lily whose eyes moved to the top of the glass display cabinet filled with books. The edge of a mahogany box could be seen resting on the top.

'My Cleopatra's dagger is up there,' Lily insisted. 'Safe and sound in a box I bought especially for it.' She pointed a shaky finger. 'It's a replica of Cleopatra's own dagger.' She gazed at Carp. 'I'm an amateur enthusiast of all things Egyptian. I have many books and papers on the subject.'

Inspector Carp put on gloves and took down the box. 'Nobody is to touch this except me. It's now evidence.'

Lily appeared unconcerned. 'I put it up there for safe-keeping.'

Fleming toyed with the top button of his tweed waistcoat, thinking several steps ahead.

'I haven't touched that box in quite some time,' Lily said. 'Valerie and I have a matching pair of Egyptian daggers. She has one while I have the other. It's highly decorative and even has a scarab beetle with brightly coloured shiny stones. It's purely ceremonial. Valerie and I both have an interest in ancient Egyptian history,' Lily said. 'The subject is how we started our friendship in the first place.'

Carp lifted the golden clasp on the dagger's mahogany case. 'We've searched Valerie Toussaint's home, where we found her dagger.' A frown formed on his face. He looked at Lily, then at Fleming. He spun the wooden box around to reveal the red silk interior.

'It's empty?' Lily exclaimed.

'Everything's going to be fine, Lily,' Fleming immediately proclaimed. 'I'll work out what all this means. You have my word.'

Lily began to tremble. 'I don't understand.'

'You're going to have to go with Inspector Carp,' Fleming said softly.

Carp took out his handcuffs, but after a discreet reassuring gesture from Fleming, he thought better of it, and put them away. Carp spoke matter-of-factly. 'Lily Riley, you're to accompany me to the police station where you will be questioned in connection with the murder of Valerie Toussaint. Do you understand?'

She nodded. 'Yes,' Lily said faintly. 'But I didn't do it.'

'This is preposterous,' Fleming insisted.

'I'm sorry, but I have no choice,' Carp continued. 'Lily, I'm now going to read you your rights.'

'He can't think I did it?' Lily said weakly. 'She was my best friend. Is there nothing you can do, Henry? If ever I needed your help, it's now.'

'Just be patient,' Fleming said. 'I'll get to the bottom of this. You have my word.' Fleming wasted no time. By using a handkerchief to avoid leaving fingerprints, he cautiously examined the mahogany box before Carp whisked it away as evidence. 'You'll find no fingerprints on the box, Inspector Carp. I can guarantee it. This box has recently been wiped clean.' He ran a finger over the top of the display cabinet which in contrast had a fine layer of dust.

'On the contrary, I expect to find Lily's. Hers and hers alone. I'm sorry, Fleming, truly. All the evidence points to her. It's clear she's guilty. My only job now is to find the murder weapon and establish a motive. I have a hunch I'll quickly discover a bitter jealousy, rivalry, or maybe the motive is greed. The usual reasons.' He sighed with satisfaction. 'As I told you, this is a simple case. All I had to do was follow the evidence.'

CHAPTER SIX

After a sleepless night, Fleming rose early and sat at the kitchen table. He'd made himself breakfast, but it remained untouched on a plate in front of him. With no appetite for food, he sipped his breakfast tea and reviewed his notes. In his hand, he toyed with a small Egyptian pyramid that he'd used as a paperweight for his scribblings.

A forlorn Kitty sat in Lily's empty armchair. From time to time she mewed pitifully.

Fleming got to his feet.

Having risen early, he'd spent a considerable amount of time polishing and shining his brown brogues in preparation for what lay ahead. He'd used that time to think. As though putting on military uniform he stood erect and buttoned a lightweight woollen blazer over his tweed waistcoat.

'I have work to do, Kitty. Lily's depending on me.'

Kitty glanced at him before looking back at the front door, where she no doubt hoped for Lily's return.

'Never fear, Kitty. I'll bring her home. You have my word.'

~

THE FIRST STOP was to interview Warren, who he'd arranged to meet on his allotment. It was a short distance so, rather than drive the Austin 7, as fun as his new little car was, Fleming decided to walk. He hadn't gone far when the vicar raised a hand to catch his attention. He appeared to have been shopping and carried a bag.

'I'm sorry to hear the police believe Lily's a suspect,' the vicar said. 'It feels like a second tragedy has befallen the village. She's always been a cherished member of my flock. I want you to know Barbara and I have prayed for her, and will continue to do so until the true culprit is revealed.'

'That's very kind, thank you.'

'Will you be staying in Fulbridge a little longer?'

'I've decided to make a few enquiries of my own.'

'That would suggest that much like myself, you feel the police have the wrong person in custody.'

Fleming chose his words carefully. 'I feel it's important to ensure the police investigation is as thorough as it can be.'

'I'm relieved to hear it. I heard from Lily about your many investigative triumphs. She's very proud of you. If there's anything I can do to help, you need only ask.'

'In that case, there is something I was wondering. What reason would there have been for Valerie to be in the church so late in the evening? I don't recall there being an evening service.'

'Valerie was a great help to me.' He placed a hand on his heart. 'On a Saturday evening, she would make sure the church was ship-shape ready for Sunday service. That will be why she was there.'

'You didn't see her yourself?'

'No. I was called away to visit a parishioner who's in the hospital. She's very ill. We prayed together.'

'How about your wife?'

'Barbara was exhausted from being on her feet all day at the fete. She was at home. I checked on her before leaving. She was fast asleep.'

'She's okay, I trust?'

He took off his heavy knit cardigan and slung it over his arm. 'She gets migraines from time to time. They're quite debilitating.'

'Can you think of anyone in particular who might have had a grudge against Valerie Toussaint?'

The vicar stepped back. 'You don't think somebody from the village could be responsible for the murder? I assumed you were considering an outsider.'

'I'm merely gathering information.'

The vicar shook his head. The shopping bag he was carrying clinked and fell open.

Fleming instinctively stepped forward to assist, but there was no need.

'It's church wine,' he explained, while adjusting his grip. 'Some medication for Barbara, too. In fact, I should be getting back to her.'

Fleming continued on his way when the vicar turned back and caught up with him again. 'Now I come to think of it, Olivia Bennett would be a good person to speak to. She and Valerie argued over the use of bunting, of all things. Valerie was opposed to hanging it from the church on fete day. I was forced to intervene when the argument became heated. As far as I'm concerned, there's no problem with a little *tasteful* bunting. I try to be open-minded, and modern, about such things.'

'I'll be sure to speak to Olivia.'

The vicar checked the time. 'I must dash, Barbara was in terrible discomfort this morning. I left her in a darkened room. I was meant to be going on a retreat but with this hanging over the village I simply can't leave, it'll have to be cancelled. And with the church being unavailable for the time being, I have letters to write and telegrams to send.'

～

THE FULBRIDGE ALLOTMENT wasn't a particularly large area, just a strip of land beside cattle-sheds. Fleming noticed a small herd of Friesian cattle up on the hill beyond the farmhouse.

Warren's plot was orderly and surprisingly lush. He was bent over sowing seeds. He wore wellington boots that he'd painted a bright orange, denim dungarees and a baby blue t-shirt. 'I won't be a moment. I'm putting in some autumn salad.'

Fleming stood beside a row of canes where he could see runner beans. He thought of Skip and how he'd have loved sniffing around on the allotment. 'You certainly have green fingers,' he said.

'I love being out here. It's good for the soul.'

'The artichokes look incredible. They're so ornate and other-worldly in appearance.'

'Aren't they a magnificent plant? They've done so well this year.' His smile quickly faded. 'I'm still in shock. I loved Valerie like a sister. And I certainly don't believe for a second Lily harmed her. How is my poor Lily? Have you spoken to her? The thought of her spending a night in a police cell makes me shudder.'

'She's as well as can be expected.'

'The poor darling.' Warren closed the door to his shed and locked it. 'You wouldn't believe the village gossip. I had to get away from it all. I despise all that tittle-tattle.'

'What sort of tittle-tattle?' Fleming asked.

'There're all kinds of speculation about why Lily might have – I shiver to even say the word – *murdered* Valerie. Not that I believe it for a second,' he added hastily. 'I mean, I think it's far more likely to have been Petunia.' He slapped a hand to his mouth. 'I'm not accusing Petunia. She's an absolute darling. But...'

'But what?'

Warren stepped closer and spoke conspiratorially. 'I saw her leaving Valerie's house in the afternoon, right after she'd withdrawn from the show. All that nonsense about her labels. I never touched her jars, and I told her so. We made up. I can give as good as I get, and my *Precious* Petunia respects that. I only call her Precious Petunia for a giggle. It's a little irony. She totally understands it. How her husband Dicky puts up with her is beyond me. He should be sainted.' He forced a nervous laugh.

'You saw her leaving Valerie's house right after she withdrew from the show?'

'I thought it was odd. Of course, she didn't really withdraw from the show.'

'No?'

'Of course not. Valerie made it clear that Petunia would be marked down on her presentation and there was nothing she could do about it. That lit Petunia's fuse. She's famous for her temper, and it didn't take long for her to explode. First at me, who she initially accused of sabotage. Then at Valerie. My goodness, they had a right old ding dong.'

'Did Petunia threaten Valerie?'

'No. Nothing like that. She wouldn't harm a fly. Petunia's all bark and no bite. She has her tantrums and then it's all over. She's like a toddler who misbehaves when she can't get her own way. It's very ugly in a grown woman, but I love her all the same. Deep down, she has a heart of gold.' Watering can in hand, he filled it from a water barrel, then gave a drink to the seeds he'd sown. 'I asked Petunia why she'd gone to Valerie's house, but she wouldn't tell me. At the time, I didn't think much of it. Now, with everything that's happened, I wonder if it might be important.'

'It could very well be. Thank you for your time,' Fleming said.

'I don't want to believe it was Petunia. But I can't

have the thought of Lily being wrongly imprisoned on my conscience.'

'I understand.'

~

PETUNIA HAD JUST RECEIVED her groceries and was tipping the delivery boy. The lad pedalled hard to get the bike moving.

Her eyes fell on Fleming. 'You're Lily's knight in shining armour, are you?'

'I'm her friend. I'm also a private detective. I hoped I might ask you a few questions.'

'I guessed as much. I suppose that's why you were listening in on the private conversation between Dicky and I at the fete.' She looked Fleming up and down, assessing him. He looked different to when she'd first seen him. It had been obvious he was a rich type, but now he also appeared commanding. 'The police think they have the case sewn up. So why're you sticking your snout in where it's not wanted? You seem to be making a habit of it.'

'Old habits die hard.'

'Interesting choice of words under the circumstances.' She stared at him flatly.

'Perhaps you're right,' Fleming said mildly.

'So what do you want? I have a busy day.'

'A few minutes of your time.'

She thought about how to respond for a moment. 'Follow me to the kitchen. Wipe your shoes. The hallway rug's new.'

Fleming did as instructed.

'Dicky's at work. He's based nearby and occasionally visits the London office.' Petunia began packing away the groceries.

'I don't have long. I'm going to the beach with friends, so what do you want from me?'

'I heard you withdrew from the show.'

She scoffed. 'What about it? You think I murdered Valerie over losing to Warren's spicy apple and walnut chutney?'

'I've known crazier motives.' Fleming's face was grave.

'When I left home, the labels on my jars were perfect. I was up until the early hours writing the damn things. I leave the box of labels for two minutes and when I return, my chances of winning have been sabotaged. Weeks, months of work, down the river. The whole day was a sham. I was squeezed onto the end of a table. Shoved into a corner. With the flower displays behind me, there was barely enough room to swing a cat. I'm not afraid to tell you that I gave Valerie a piece of my mind. I didn't mince my words.'

'From what I hear, you have quite a temper.'

'I was annoyed. As I'm sure most people would be.'

'Did you threaten her?'

'I didn't *threaten* her. I really don't care about jam, or preserves, or any of that. I took part in their miserable little fete because I'm trying to fit into village life. I went to a lot of effort and I feel the least she could have done was given me some leeway.' Petunia paused for a moment, took a deep breath. 'I'm fiery. I speak my mind. I don't suffer fools.' She looked Fleming up and down. 'I don't care who they are. Some people don't like that.'

'Why did you go to Valerie's house on the afternoon of the fete?'

'I didn't.' She turned her back on him and put some flour and tea in the pantry.

'A witness saw you leaving her house shortly after your argument with her.'

Petunia slammed the pantry door shut. 'It's not what you think.'

'At the moment, I think nothing. I'm open-minded. Curious.'

She poured them both a glass of water and perched on a stool. 'I'm ashamed of what I did. I want you to understand that. As I told you, I get cross, and I see red. Since I was a little girl, it's always been the same. I have outbursts. I'd never hurt anyone. I get frustrated.

It builds up and up, and I vent. People annoy me. That's all. Dicky's the only person who can calm me. When I'm alone with him, it's like I'm a different person.'

'Explain to me what happened,' Fleming said soothingly.

'Valerie's a big fan of Egyptian history. She and Lily have this absurd obsession with pharaohs and mummies, pyramids and all that nonsense. It's a bit wacky if you ask me. They're grown women, for goodness' sake.'

Fleming nodded encouragingly. 'You were going to explain why you went to her home.'

'I'm getting to it.' She took a deep breath. 'Right after you eavesdropped on my conversation, I walked over to her cottage. It's like a museum with all the books, artefacts and junk everywhere. Her garden's mainly fruit trees, vegetables and noisy chickens. There's also a small part of the garden given over to flowers, common in Egypt apparently. At the centre there's a small pyramid and a weird winged lion with a woman's head. I forget what it's called. She did tell me once, but I wasn't interested enough to remember.'

'The Great Sphinx?'

Petunia snapped her fingers. 'That's it. She had her own miniature versions done out of topiary.' Petunia's face flushed red. She sipped her cool water. 'I destroyed them with a pair of secateurs I found on the table behind me at the fete. The gentleman there was exhibiting flowers.' She leaned back in her seat. 'I regret it now. Obviously, it was childish of me.'

'That was the reason you went to her cottage?'

'Yes.' She frowned.

'You didn't go inside the cottage?'

'No. Did you think I went there to harm her? If you did, you're really clutching at straws.'

'Where did you go after that?'

'I went back to the fete. Carried on like nothing happened.'

'Can anyone vouch for that?'

'Loads of people. Ask around.'

'How about at the time of the murder?'

'I was with Dicky. We had dinner. Then we went for an evening walk down by the river. People must have seen us. We saw Warren. I think he saw us, though I can't be sure. When we realised something had happened at the church, we took a look.'

'I see.'

'You thought I had something to do with her murder? Now what do you think?'

'I think to arrive at the truth, it's important to assemble all the facts, even the small details that at first appear insignificant.'

Petunia looked pleased to have disappointed him. 'This village is full of liars, but I'm not one of them. As far as I'm concerned, we'd all know where we stood if more people minded their own business. Instead, the folks in this place scurry around with their secrets, talking behind one another's backs, casting aspersions, while pretending they're all prim and proper. There's plenty that goes on in Fulbridge that people don't want out in the open.'

'Such as?'

'Well, the vicar's wife, for one. She thinks she's mightier than thou. Looking down her nose at all and sundry because her husband's the vicar. And his flock goes along with it. Blind to the truth. But I know her secret.'

'What secret is that, Petunia?'

'She's a drunk. She hides it well but I recognise the signs.'

'You're sure?'

'Certain.' She folded her arms with satisfaction. 'Not as saintly as you thought now, is she?'

Fleming rose to leave and Petunia showed him to the door. 'Sorry,' she said. 'I know I can be prickly. I carry a lot of baggage from my past.'

'Apology accepted,' Fleming said. 'One small thing before I leave.'

'Yes?'

'Your labels. Did you ever consider the person behind you at the show, the gentleman exhibiting his flowers? He might have sprayed his display to freshen it up and inadvertently caused the damage?'

Fleming buttoned his jacket and headed to his next stop.

CHAPTER SEVEN

The vicar put down his pen and examined his correspondence. He'd sent telegrams earlier to postpone church functions for the week ahead. Two weddings and a christening. Feeling fatigued, he closed his eyes and allowed himself a moment of silent contemplation.

As sleep began to overwhelm him, there was a knocking at the front door. He groaned to himself, then moved quickly to avoid the visitor knocking again.

'Twice in one day,' the vicar said. 'To what do I owe the honour?'

Fleming smiled apologetically. 'I wondered if I might speak to your wife?'

'Barbara's sleeping,' the vicar said. After a moment's pause, he added, 'What am I thinking?

Come in. Perhaps I can help? I was just about to make a pot of tea. I also have some pear tart that's been calling to me.'

'That would be most welcome.'

They took their tea and tart at a small table in the courtyard garden at the back of the vicarage. The garden was well established and bursting with colour. A pear tree that looked as old as the cottage laboured under branches full of pears that had recently become ready to pick.

There was a pergola at the far end of the garden with a wooden bench. In the centre of the small lawn a water-well sat. On top of it lay a cast iron sheet, which was padlocked for safety.

Fleming walked along the garden borders and admired the plants. He stopped to smell a pink rose. 'The perfume's magical.'

'I love roses. There's a purity about them. You should smell this variety.' The vicar took Fleming to the pergola, where a white rambling rose was covered in bloom.

'Of all the plants in my own garden, roses are my favourite,' Fleming said. He then turned his attention back to the well. 'Is it full of water?'

'Yes. But it's no longer safe to drink. The cover was fitted to the well before we arrived. When my nephew and niece were young, it was essential. They were a bit of a handful and would run riot in the garden.' He laughed heartily.

The two men returned to the small table where they sat down.

'How's your investigation going? Have you made any headway?' The vicar's long face looked tired.

'I have theories which I'm working through, but it's early days. As I'm sure you can imagine, there's a lot to consider. It's important to be thorough in such matters.'

'In my job, I can tell when something's bothering a person.' The vicar could see Fleming was reticent about asking a question. 'If I had to guess, I'd say it's to do with Barbara.'

'You're an astute man,' Fleming said as he stirred his tea. 'It's a delicate matter.'

'Tongues have been wagging.' The vicar leaned back in his seat; looked skyward as his eyes brimmed. He took a moment to compose himself. 'I'd rather what I'm about to tell you went no further.'

'You have my word.'

The vicar spent a moment choosing his words. 'Barbara has a sickness. It's a curse.'

'I see.'

'It's not her fault, you understand. There's nobody to blame.'

'I'm sorry. How are you both coping?'

'That's the burning question, isn't it? If I'm being perfectly honest, we're not. Each day's a struggle and mostly I'm in denial. That's often how men cope, I think. They bury their heads in the sand and hope all will be well.'

'I understand. What we can't fix, we try to put out of our mind.'

Jonathan's voice faltered. 'Once again today, we've rowed. She's cried. I've stormed out. I know I should be stronger and I pray daily for strength, greater under-standing and compassion, but when all is said and done, I'm just a man. Flesh and blood.'

'You're an amazing man,' Barbara stated.

The two men turned in surprise.

'I didn't know you were standing there, my love,' the vicar said. He got to his feet, put his arms around his wife and hugged her. 'How are you, darling?'

Fleming, who also stood, moved to a different seat at the table so Barbara could sit beside her husband.

'I'm tired of all the secrets,' Barbara said. 'Ask me whatever you need to, Mr Fleming. Valerie's gone. Lily accused of her murder. It's time I confessed to my part in all this. None of us in the village can claim to be wholly innocent.'

The vicar held his wife's trembling hands and comforted her as she explained.

Barbara spoke softly. 'I was a keen walker for

many years. The countryside around Fulbridge is glorious. I was out on one of my afternoon walks when I slipped on a rock and twisted my knee. At first, I thought nothing of it and, though it was painful, I fully expected that after some rest, it would recover. Unfortunately, it didn't, and eventually I went to our doctor who prescribed morphine and offered treatment.'

'That's how it started,' the vicar said.

'I had surgery on the knee and it improved things to a degree. It's painful and swells after a long day on my feet. The other problem, however, is that I found myself addicted to the medication. If I ran out of morphine, I'd become unbearable. Eventually, Jonathan cottoned on to my addiction and, with the doctor's help, weaned me off the stuff.'

'And that's when you substituted the morphine for alcohol?' Fleming asked.

'Yes.' Barbara nodded.

'It was a lucky guess. I detected you weren't well but, until now, hadn't decided in what way.' He turned to Jonathan. 'In your shopping bag this morning, when it fell open, I happened to notice it was regular white wine, not red, for the altar wine. Which means it wasn't for the church, as you suggested. Unless you were hiding something, there was no reason to lie.'

Barbara wiped away her tears with a handkerchief.

'I really don't know how Jonathan copes with me. Most days I'm intolerable.'

'God never gives us more than we can handle,' the vicar said. 'We'll get through this.'

'I try,' Barbara said. 'Every day, I try.'

Fleming waited an appropriate moment before returning to formalities. 'I'm sorry to have to ask, but where were you both at the time of the murder?'

The vicar scratched his head. 'Let me think. The fete ran from one to five p.m. I helped clear up for about an hour or so afterwards. I came home and had a spot of dinner. Then I checked on Barbara, who was fast asleep. I left for the hospital to pray with an elderly parishioner. I stayed for roughly an hour at the hospital and got back to the village at eight thirty p.m. That was when I came upon the incident at the church and found Lily in an awful state. I comforted her and others, and we prayed, until the police arrived.'

Fleming turned to Barbara. 'My apologies, but I must ask.'

'It's quite all right. It had been a particularly horrible day. My spat with Petunia was all the excuse I needed to open a bottle. I wanted to block it out. I came home early at around four p.m. One drink led to another and another. Eventually, I blacked out and slept until Jonathan woke me in the morning to tell me the terrible news.'

'There's no point in me trying to wake her,' the vicar explained. 'The drink makes her insensible.'

'You heard nothing of the disturbance, Mrs Ardern?'

'I'm sorry. I knew nothing of what happened until Jonathan informed me this morning. I'd been tired and irritable at the fete. It made me short-tempered with Petunia, and others too. Valerie wanted to talk to me, and I told her I didn't have time. If I'd been less worried about myself and had found the time, she might still be alive.' Barbara sobbed.

'You don't know that for sure,' the vicar said.

'Do you have any idea what Valerie wanted to talk to you about?' Fleming asked.

Barbara shook her head. 'I can only assume it was to do with the money.'

Fleming frowned. 'Money?'

Barbara looked surprised. 'You didn't know? The village has sold jam and chutney locally for quite some time. I had the idea of selling the products further afield. Large towns and cities for example. Valerie took charge and corresponded with some buyers. Then out of the blue, there was interest from Whittingworth Foods.'

'They have offices in London and New York,' the vicar added. 'The Whittingworth family have been in shipping for years.'

'That's very interesting,' Fleming said. 'Lily never mentioned a word of this to me.'

'Lily's a conservative woman, with admirably high standards,' the vicar said. 'She's never been one to speak of money. In fact, I always found she actively shied away from the topic. I think she considers talk of wealth as rather undignified.'

'Money can do a lot of good when it's in the right hands. Wouldn't you agree, Mr Fleming?' suggested Barbara.

'Most definitely,' Fleming said. 'Thank you for your time and the tea. I'll be on my way.'

'You're welcome to stay for dinner,' Barbara said.

'That's very kind, but I must get back. I'm cat-sitting Kitty, and I'm sure the poor little mite must be starving by now. Perhaps, another time?'

'Of course. You're always welcome,' the vicar said.

∽

BACK AT THE cottage with Kitty fed and watered, Fleming examined the pantry and realised there was no dinner for himself. Having exhausted all the food cupboards, it was clear he would also need provisions for both himself and Kitty over the coming days.

Thirty minutes later, he was standing outside the recently opened fish and chip shop waiting for his order to be prepared. In the front basket of Lily's bicycle was a bag of groceries, and two whole mackerel for Kitty.

'Great minds think alike,' Keith Bennett said. His soft features were full of colour from cycling the winding roads to the town chip shop. 'When you're tired and hungry, it's hard to beat a fish and chip supper, laden with salt and soaked in vinegar.'

'I'll be perfectly honest,' said Fleming. 'I've not eaten fish and chips out of a newspaper before but I've been excited to try it.'

The two men chuckled.

Keith ordered his fish supper and joined Fleming outside to wait. 'Word's out you're running your own investigation into what happened to Valerie. Olivia would have my guts for garters if I neglected to enquire how it was going?' He dabbed the perspiration on his brow and neck with a purple handkerchief.

'It's a puzzle at the moment. I'm examining all the pieces and wondering how they fit together. It could be that you can help?'

'If I can, I'd be delighted. I've dreamt of becoming a world famous detective.' His kindly eyes shone with delight. 'I didn't know her well, but from what I did know of her, I can tell you Valerie was an angel. One of the most caring people I've ever met. Such a big heart and gentle soul.'

They collected their food orders, and together the two men cycled back to the village. They stopped outside Keith and Olivia's cottage. 'You've been extremely helpful and corroborated many of the things I was told today. I also wondered how well Olivia knew Valerie?'

'As a school teacher for many years, Livvy knows practically everyone. She also feels it's important to be involved in parish council matters. She's active in so many things.'

'What about yourself? Do you get involved?'

'Me? No. I have a hard enough time earning a crust and the upkeep of the cottage and garden. Especially with all the little jobs Livvy drags me into.' He chuckled. 'You saw me hammering in all those little signs for the village fete. That's just the tip of the iceberg. I was up at the crack of dawn and working all day. It was exhausting work and if it wasn't for Valerie, who brought me refreshments, like my very own Florence Nightingale, I might have had a turn. She was a very thoughtful woman.'

Olivia came to the window of the cottage and waved.

'I'd better go,' Keith said with a wide smile. 'We don't want cold fish.'

Fleming was about to leave when he decided to

mention the garden. 'Beautiful roses,' he said. 'Not a blemish on them and so full of flowers.'

'You should come back in the morning. It's hard to appreciate them in this light.'

'You obviously know your roses.'

'They're a particular favourite. These yellow ones have a fabulous fragrance. They make wonderful cuttings. We have a bouquet inside in a vase.' He gently held a rose head and inhaled its perfume. 'Valerie loved this particular rose. She often told me how she'd catch the scent in the air as she passed the cottage.' His voice breaking, he added, 'I keep expecting her to appear. I still see her everywhere I look.' His hands tightly grasped the bag of fish and chips. 'Excuse me.' He rushed inside the house without a backward glance.

CHAPTER EIGHT

It had been several days since Valerie's murder and Lily's hasty arrest. Though he was averse to saying as much, Fleming was becoming increasingly frustrated with Inspector Carp's stubbornness. It was because of that pig-headedness that he insisted on regularly visiting the police station to discuss the investigation with him.

Once again, he found they were unable to agree. Unfortunately, Carp still considered Lily his prime suspect, and due to the severity of the crime, he had decided she should remain in custody.

Arriving back at the cottage, it surprised Fleming to find Olivia Bennett waiting for him.

'Good afternoon, Mrs Bennett,' Fleming said.

'Please call me Olivia or Livvy. I'm aware you're

keen to speak to me and I feel awful that I've put you off until now. The whole horrid event left me feeling shaken to my soul. I know Keith has been his usual affable self and was no doubt helpful, but I'm well aware that information directly from the horse's mouth, so to speak, is always the most valuable, and so here I am, at your disposal.' She gave a sniffling laugh. 'I thought perhaps we might go for a drive.' She eyed Fleming's shiny motorcar. 'I've made a picnic. I know a wonderful spot beside the river. It's private and far away from prying eyes.'

'That's a very attractive idea,' Fleming said. Out of habit, he checked the time on his pocket watch and made a mental note. 'I would be delighted.'

$\sim$

THE PAIR SAT at a picnic blanket on the tranquil bend of a river. Willow trees draped their branches into the slow-moving water. A grey heron stood motionless in the shallows as it waited for fish to swim too close. A kingfisher flashed low across the water like an electric blue dart. In the distance, boys and girls swung from a rope tied to a branch that overhung the river while, further on, another group jumped from a bridge into the water, daring one another to somersault and flip.

Mrs Olivia Bennett was a handsome woman, although not a natural beauty like Valerie Toussaint. She worked a little harder to accentuate her fine qualities. Her attractiveness was mostly hidden behind a tough veneer and forthright demeanour and was only revealed when the facade slipped and she accidentally smiled.

'Won't you have a piece of carrot cake, Henry?' She slid a large slice in front of him before he had time to answer. 'You don't mind me calling you Henry, do you? Mr Fleming seems so formal.'

'Henry's absolutely fine. The cake looks delicious. I can manage a little. After all, you went to so much trouble.' He tasted the cake and made the appropriate appreciative noises. Putting down his cake fork, he said, 'There's the possibility that a terrible miscarriage of justice could befall our good friend Lily.'

'I couldn't agree more, Henry. How can I help?'

Fleming felt sure Mrs Bennett would skirt around the subject unless he was direct. 'When did you first become aware of your husband's infatuation with Valerie Toussaint?'

Olivia hardly flinched. 'Like most men, Keith's head is easily turned. It's happened since the dawn of time. It's not his fault. She was... Under the circumstances, I'd rather not give my honest opinion. In Keith's head, he thought it was something more than it was. In his naivety, he actually told her how he felt. The fool was shattered when she rejected him. His male ego crushed underfoot like a cigarette butt.'

'As painful as it was for him, I'm sure you were equally hurt when you found out?'

'Of course I was hurt. We made a commitment to one another.' She needlessly shuffled the cutlery in the picnic basket. 'His foolish declaration was many months ago. We're over it now.'

'How did you find out?' Fleming asked.

'She told me.' Olivia's lower lip quivered. 'I cringe when I think of it. For all his failings, I love Keith dearly. I know him better than he knows himself.'

'How did Keith react to be being turned down?'

'He didn't become maniacal and harm her, if that's what you're thinking.'

'You know that for certain?'

'Well… no. But you've met the man. He's harmless. A gentle soul. I've often thought Keith's like a tortoise. When things get stormy or uncertain, he pulls his head in and hides. He retreats into his shell until he senses the coast is clear.'

'How did he react to her murder? When I met him, he appeared to have put a brave face on things.'

'That's Keith, through and through. He doesn't want to hurt my feelings, so he messes around in his garden and pretends like nothing ever happened. He most likely believes he'll wake up tomorrow, and find it was all a bad dream. That she'll be waiting for him with open arms. I'm not sure how I feel. But he's my Keith. Inside, I'm certain he's pining for her and blaming himself for her death, and I have to live with that. Time will heal us. I'm sure of it.'

'Why would he blame himself?' Fleming asked.

Olivia shrugged. 'For the same reason others in this village feel responsible. You can't swing a cat around here without hitting someone with a skeleton in their cupboard.'

'What about you?'

She raised her elegant chin. 'It would seem I'm the exception to that rule.' She corrected a lock of hair that had been caught by a gentle breeze.

'Where were you at the time of the murder?' Fleming asked with sensitivity.

She chuckled 'There it is. My undoing.' Olivia's facade faded. 'It seems my alibi relies on revealing a secret I'd rather remained hidden. You'll find out sooner or later, so I may as well make a clean breast of it.'

Fleming had guessed Olivia had brought him somewhere quiet for a reason, and now he would learn the truth, or some version of it. 'It's always better to get these things out in the open. I would encourage you to speak truthfully and allow me to hear your side first.'

'I haven't told the police, but I feel I can trust you, Henry.'

'I'm only interested in finding Valerie's killer.'

She briefly paused, as though summoning courage. 'At the time of the murder, I was with a gentleman friend. We meet once a week for tea and biscuits. He lives in the next village.'

'I see,' Fleming said.

'I don't think you do. Men always jump to the wrong conclusion.'

'You meet for tea and biscuits?'

'Yes. It's all purely innocent. A man and a woman can be friends, and nothing more.'

'Of course.'

'He's a widower. We talk. Sometimes he'll talk and I'll sit and knit. It's about having company, especially for him.'

'Keith is unaware?' Fleming asked softly. 'You hide this from him?'

'It's not that I haven't told Keith on purpose. I'm concerned he might misunderstand our simple friendship. He'd jump to the wrong conclusion. Accuse me of heaven knows what. My point is that I'm trying to say my friendship is nothing like Keith's infatuation was with Valerie.' She sighed. 'Why does life have to be so complicated?'

'How did you meet your friend?'

'At the local tennis club. I go there twice a month for tea with girlfriends.'

'What's the gentleman's name? I should speak to him to corroborate your alibi.'

'I'd rather not say. I know that puts me in a spot, but he's a very private man. To avoid gossip, we meet at a discreet little teashop near Pennyworth Cove. We talk about all sorts. He's very educated. Knows a lot about politics, and current affairs, literature, history and he's extremely well-travelled. He and his late wife toured all around the British Isles. He misses her so much. Having someone to talk to is such a small thing that we take for granted. When it's gone, missing from your life, it's suddenly all you think about. I try to be that person to him. I enjoy being an ear for him. He looks forward to our meetings. Can you understand?'

'I certainly can.'

'We usually meet during the day. It's more appropriate. On this occasion, he was feeling rather down and I agreed to meet him a little later than usual. I made an excuse to Keith and travelled to a little restaurant where I listened and he talked. I feel sure it helped.'

Fleming thanked Olivia for her candour. 'It's fair

to say you're dealing with a lot right now. I hope you and Keith are able to talk things through. Out of interest, which month did you marry?'

Olivia looked surprised by the question. 'April. We had a spring wedding.'

'A romantic time of year to be married. Warm weather, cherry blossom, and blooming flowers.'

Olivia nodded in agreement but said nothing more.

~

WARREN SILVERS PUT down the telegram and clapped his hands with joy.

'Good news?' Fleming asked.

'Wonderful news,' Warren replied. 'The client's delighted and will be picking it up at the end of the week.'

He pointed to a large oil painting standing against the wall in his studio. The picture was of a barefoot woman on a golden sandy beach. The sand glittered and actually appeared to be gold leaf. The subject's lightweight dress flowed. It was transparent in places against the evening light and revealed her figure while retaining all modesty. She was throwing a stick for a small dog, which had leapt into the air to catch it. The image was full of vivid colours that fought for attention. The fiery sunset in the background drew the eye beyond the immediate action of the woman and the dog.

'You're a talented man,' Fleming said.

The canvas was surrounded by smaller canvases of varying sizes. Mostly landscapes, but also portraits all in similarly striking, vibrant colours.

'Feel free to browse. There are plenty here that need to find homes.'

'I might just do that.' Fleming's eyes were drawn to the image of a woman sitting alone at a window. It was one of the few paintings that was done in muted tones of greys and blues. Her eyes stared into the distance and Fleming wondered if she was waiting for someone's return.

'You like that one?' Warren asked.

'It's full of questions,' Fleming said. 'I sense there's a lot going on in her mind. She's completely absorbed in her own world. The blurred background suggests a dream, or feeling lost; the lack of clarity in her thoughts.'

Warren smiled. 'That's the beauty of a piece like this. It can mean whatever the beholder wants it to mean.'

'Does she have a name?'

Warren shook his head. 'No.' He picked up the painting and handed it to Fleming. 'Take it. Hang it in your home and if you decide to keep her, you can make me an offer.'

'I couldn't do that,' Fleming said. 'Let me think about it. I shan't forget her. She reminds me of someone I once knew. Someone dear to me.'

CHAPTER NINE

Fleming poured a cup of breakfast tea. He was in fine spirits. He'd had a good night's sleep and then gone out early. He'd taken a trip to the tennis club where a few discreet questions had proven extremely useful.

There was a knock at the back door and the vicar poked his head in. 'I hope I'm not intruding. I thought I'd check in on you.' He leaned his bicycle against the cottage wall.

Fleming poured a cup of tea for the vicar, and the pair sat in a sunny spot in the back garden. A robin seemed curious and flew close to the two men. The vicar put out a hand to see whether the bird would sit on it, but seeing no food in the open hand, it flew off to sit in the neighbour's apple tree.

'They can be so bold,' the vicar said. 'Sometimes,

the little chap in our garden gets so close that when I'm digging, I have to be careful where I plant the fork.' He chuckled to himself. 'Of course, I didn't come here to talk about our feathered friends. I'm concerned about Lily. I was wondering how your investigation was going? I'm sure you can't divulge too much, but I'm keen to know whether you're close to clearing her name and putting the real perpetrator behind bars?'

Fleming sat back in his chair and straightened his cufflinks. 'As a private detective, I am duty bound, much like the police themselves, to keep certain pieces of information close to my chest.'

'I completely understand,' the vicar said, 'but...'

'That said, without mentioning any names, I've been able to rule out several suspects and have narrowed my investigation. The task I now face is gathering sufficient evidence to present to Inspector Carp.'

'Really?' The vicar looked shocked. 'I had no idea you'd make such short work of it. It's all rather fascinating.'

'It's a matter of training the eye and mind. I've dedicated my life to the pursuit of identifying then aligning truth in all its forms.'

The vicar's eyes widened. 'How exciting.'

Fleming rose to his feet and strode a few paces away. With his back turned to the vicar, he said, 'Before visiting me this morning you went to the bakery where you purchased a large freshly baked white loaf.'

'Good heavens, that's remarkable,' the vicar said.

'It was a simple observation. On your black woollen jumper you have white flour on the underside of your arm, suggesting at some point today you've carried a loaf of bread. When at your home recently I observed a white bloomer that you'd almost finished and the crust of another still wrapped in a brown paper bag suggesting it's the preferred choice of both yourself and Mrs Ardern.'

The vicar shook his head in disbelief. 'Bravo. Keep going.'

'You've recently been to the police station and spoken to Inspector Carp. If I had to guess, I'd say it was within the last forty-eight hours.'

'Miraculous! How could you possible know that?'

'You've not once asked after Lily's well-being and, as I know you to be a good friend of hers and concerned for her health and state-of-mind, it's my belief you're already informed and therefore in no need of any further clarification on her status from myself.'

'Ingenious. And quite true.'

'Last, and by no means least, you were due home several minutes ago. You have an important engagement you're meant to attend, and it's slipped your mind.'

'The vicar jumped to his feet and checked the time on his wristwatch. You're right, I have a young couple who would like me to marry them. I'm almost ten minutes late. How on earth did you know I was late for an appointment?'

'Quite simple. I can see your wife walking at quite a pace towards this cottage. She's also very clearly agitated while in search of you!'

Fleming and the vicar both laughed. 'Outstanding! If you'll forgive me, I'd better dash.'

Fleming watched as the vicar collected his bike and joined his wife, who together headed at a quick march back to the vicarage.

Kitty jumped up on the low garden wall and pressed herself against Fleming. He stroked her. 'I presume you're wondering how I knew about the bread and his visiting Lily.

'Don't believe in my incredible powers of deduction? You want the truth?'

Kitty purred.

'On my return from the tennis club this morning, I observed the vicar queuing outside the bakery for his fresh loaf. From the traces of flour under his arm, I guessed he walked with the loaf tucked under it. As for his knowing the current status of Lily, well, that's easy. When I called the station last evening, I was told Inspector Carp was unable to come to the phone because he was with the vicar. It wasn't too much of a stretch to surmise that whatever the reason for the two of them speaking, the vicar would at some point ask after Lily, and possibly pray with her.'

Kitty rubbed her head against Fleming and he kissed her head. 'Admit it. You're impressed by my parlour tricks for the vicar. Stick with me, Kitty, and we might just make a real life detective out of you yet.'

~

PENNYWORTH COVE IS an hour's drive from Fulbridge. On a map, it appears very close and only takes so long to reach due to the many narrow and winding country roads that must be navigated to reach the secluded bay. The cove's natural and historic beauty is worth the effort. The view is breathtaking from the near-vertical chalk cliffs above the bay where sits a tea shop and a souvenir shop. Clear blue waters kiss the pebble beach. It had been one of Valerie's favourite places to visit.

It was late evening and residents of Fulbridge, neighbours, friends and family had gathered on the beach to commemorate her life. Drinks and food had been carried down the well-worn path, and a bonfire lit to signify Valerie's light and warmth.

Fleming had been invited, despite his association

with the person some vehemently believed to be responsible for Valerie's murder. He stood alone as speeches came to an end and a toast was made. There were tears and hugs and words of consolation.

'It's all rather sad, Fleming,' Dicky Longbottom said. 'Such a beauty to be snuffed out like that.'

'I sense from your tone you weren't a fan of Valerie Toussaint?' Fleming said.

'I wouldn't put it that way. She had her qualities, but she could be rather mischievous, too. She was also a thorn in my Petunia's side. From the few times I met her, I found her to be someone who liked to get her own way. Rather domineering at times and something of a force to be reckoned with. From what I heard, she was due to come into a great deal of money. Could be tens of thousands of pounds, eventually. With her death, and Lily being her business partner, it was all due to go to Lily. Some are saying that's quite a motive for snuffing her out.'

'What do you say?' Fleming asked.

'I don't have an opinion. I thought you should know, that's all. Did you also hear that Lily was reluctant to get involved? Without her recipe and face on the label, there was no deal. That meant Valerie could wave goodbye to the windfall she was hoping for.'

'Valerie had the appearance of a wealthy woman.'

Dicky tapped a finger on the side of his nose. 'Aha!

That's the impression she gave. She was once a wealthy woman, but it seems she lost it all. Her husband took her life savings and disappeared abroad with a young filly. Classic mid-life crisis, if you ask me.'

'A tragic cliché.'

'Exactly. She was left with nothing but a small pension. And she was lucky to have that by the time her lousy ex-husband had finished with her.'

'The poor woman. So much heartache.'

'From what I can work out, it made her desperate. She badgered Lily half to death until she finally agreed to do the deal. It must have frustrated her that Lily wasn't interested in money. Who can blame her? A woman her age, living comfortably, having left the limelight once, being dragged back into it again.'

'That's an interesting perspective.' Fleming sipped his hot tea.

'Not drinking the beer, Fleming?' Dicky raised his pint.

'I rarely drink alcohol. I like to keep a clear head at all times.'

'Unlike you, I don't need such clarity of mind and enjoy nothing more than a belly full of beer.' He laughed raucously.

'I get the impression Petunia isn't a fan of Fulbridge village?'

'She mentioned that the two of you spoke,' Dicky

confessed. 'In which case, I see no harm in telling you that she's hated this place since the moment we arrived. I thought life in a quintessentially English village would be an absolute dream come true for her. It turns out you can take the girl out of the city, but you simply cannot take the city out of the girl.' He slapped Fleming on the back and guffawed.

'Home is where the heart is, as they say.'

'You're right. The only person she'll miss when we leave will be Warren. Despite the fact they argue most of the time, they seem to understand one another. If it wasn't for him, I think she'd have moved back to London a long time ago. Left me to follow her like a love-sick puppy.' He let out one of his ear-splitting laughs. 'I would too. I'd follow that girl to the ends of the earth. She's spirited and she keeps me on my toes, but I'd lay down my life for her.'

Fleming chuckled. 'It makes me happy to see someone so in love.'

'I'll drink to that!' Dicky raised his glass. He drank the rest of the pint down in one and went to find another.

THERE WAS a cool breeze off the sea and Warren Silvers raised his hand to the flames while he stared at the bonfire, which crackled and hissed.

'Mesmerising, isn't it?' Olivia Bennett said.

Warren looked up. 'I suppose so.'

'Hard to believe she's gone.'

Warren looked around. 'What do you want, Olivia?'

'Nothing.'

'Then leave me alone.'

'I'm warming my hands, the same as you.'

'I know what you're doing. I told you I won't say anything.'

'As I explained to you, there's nothing to say and that's the end of it.'

'I want to be left alone.' Warren turned to walk away.

Olivia grabbed his arm. '*There's nothing to say,*' she repeated insistently.

Warren pulled away and stormed off.

Fleming approached the other side of the fire. He rubbed his hands together and held them to the warming glow. 'Is everything okay between you and Warren?'

'He's upset. We all are.' Olivia smiled, turned away. 'Excuse me.' She left Fleming standing alone.

CHAPTER TEN

The church bells rang to mark the end of service, and Fleming filed out of church with the other parishioners. He had intended to speak to Olivia, but Petunia had other ideas.

'Look at you, Mr Fleming,' Petunia said. 'Shoes like mirrors and your navy suit freshly pressed. Those trouser creases are like knives. You make quite an impression.'

'I enjoy the feel of a good suit. I no longer have an official uniform and so I make do.'

'Were you a military man?'

'I was an officer in France. Also, a policeman.' He pushed his shoulders back. 'I feel comfortable with the formality of such clothing.'

'Did I hear you say you were in France?' Dicky

asked. He put an arm around Petunia. 'Did you see much action?'

'Dicky, you shouldn't ask such questions.'

Fleming grimaced. 'It's okay. My military days were, for the most part, uneventful. I've seen more *action*, as you put it, as a private detective.'

'You know, I really would like to hear some of your stories. Why don't you join us today?'

'That's a wonderful idea,' Petunia said. 'We're visiting antique shops.'

'We're bargain hunters,' Dicky said. 'Not very good ones, mind you.'

'We go as often as we can.' Petunia held up her garnet and diamond ring. 'Dicky bought me this last time.'

'That was hardly a bargain. The shop owner was as sharp as they come. He almost had the shirt off my back. I wasn't going to blink first, and neither was he. I'll be more prudent next time.'

'You complain too much, darling. And anyway, I'm worth every penny.' She kissed him.

'So will you come, Fleming?' Dicky asked.

'I'm not sure,'

Petunia grabbed his arm. 'Please come. I've heard you're ever so clever. I'd love to see if you can spot a bargain. It'll also give me a chance to prove to you I can be adorable.'

Fleming raised his hands in submission. 'Okay. If you're serious. But on the condition that you allow me to buy our lunch.'

'Deal,' Dicky said quickly.

∿

THE ANTIQUES SHOP was in fact three huge barns filled from floor to ceiling with curiosities and wonders from all around the world. It felt as though it was possible that anything one was searching for might be found inside. From theatrical props to military uniforms, children's toys to antique clothing, clocks to signage and furniture to fishing tackle all mixed together from every decade and in no readily discernible order. It was quite mind-boggling. For bargain hunters and antiquity buffs, it was heaven.

While Petunia and Dicky scoured the barns in an excited frenzy, Fleming took a more sedate approach, and after an hour or so, he found a way to pass the time by reading old books. He dusted a seat to avoid dirtying his trousers and rested on what he thought might have once been a row of plush theatre seats. They appeared to be fire damaged.

'Are you okay there?' Petunia called. She emerged beside two mannequins dressed as Roman centurions, complete with shields and swords.

Fleming held up a leather-bound copy of *Pride and Prejudice*. 'I'm perfectly fine, thank you.'

'It's like an Aladdin's cave in here.'

Before he could reply, she was gone. Fleming put down the book and examined some walking canes. He wasn't in need of a stick, yet, but they were quite attractive and perhaps one day he might. He selected one with a brass knob handle. It seemed curious. He twisted the top and found it turned. He removed the knob's cap. Inside the cap was a compass. Inside the top of the long cane, and the remainder of the knob, was a thin silver tube. He removed the tube from inside the cane and examined it. It had a flip cap lid. Upon further inspection, he suspected it might be for a dram of whisky. He was weighing up whether the cane might be a good investment when a glint of golden metal caught his eye.

Fleming removed a wooden box full of toy railway tracks and parts to reveal an open leather chest. Arranged neatly was a top hat, a suit jacket with tails, trousers, white gloves, and a cloak. Laid on top was a magician's magic wand. Beneath the clothes were chains and a large padlock. It had been the shiny collapsible birdcage that had caught his eye. He examined the items that had once belonged to a magician with interest. He tried on the top hat. It was too small. Examining it, he found a secret chamber, inside of which were colourful silk scarves. He began pulling them out. Having removed the scarves, he realised the chamber was big enough to hold a small animal like a dove. He turned the hat around in his hands. Pushing from the top and bottom, he was able to collapse the hat, so it laid flat. With a flourish and a flick of the wrist, the hat popped back up.

'What have you found there?' Dicky asked. He pulled out the cloak and threw it over his shoulders.

'Very dashing,' Petunia said.

'It's everything one would need to become a magician. Let's see if we can find something to make Petunia vanish,' Dicky teased.

Fleming dropped the top hat and sat down, suddenly silent. His left hand went to his waistcoat's left pocket and, in a circular motion, his thumb rubbed the pocket watch inside.

'Are you okay?' Dicky asked. 'You look awfully pale.'

'I've been so foolish and so blind. I'm afraid we must leave at once.'

'Of course. We can do lunch another day.'

'I'm so sorry. I'll make it up to you.' Fleming marched out of the barn with Petunia and Dicky barely able to keep up. 'I must return to the cottage immediately.'

FLEMING PACED BACK and forth outside Lily's cottage. Inside, constables searched each room. An exasperated Inspector Carp came out of the front door. 'Before you say anything, I have no choice, Fleming. The murder weapon is somewhere in this cottage, I'm certain of it, and my officers will find it. These old cottages date back hundreds of years to a time when valuable items were stashed under floorboards, behind bookcases, and in false walls. There's even talk of a secret chamber beneath the church and treasure stashed inside coffins in the churchyard. Back in the day, if you wanted to hide something, or someone, from the authorities, then the builders of these old cottages made it possible.'

'You won't find it here. You're wasting precious time,' Fleming said angrily. 'It's beyond me that you won't listen to reason.'

'I *have* listened and you're not making any sense. All this talk of magic tricks, Houdini, vanishing rabbits and the like. From what I understand, and correct me if I'm wrong, you're telling me the real killer vanished into thin air?' Inspector Carp pinched the bridge of his nose. 'I suppose there was a puff of smoke too? It seems to me you've lost your touch.'

'Let me explain it to you again.'

'It doesn't matter how many times you explain it. I'm only interested in evidence and proof. When my officers find the murder weapon here in Lily's cottage, I'll have all I need.'

'What evidence have your officers come up with so far, may I ask?'

'In truth, they've been at it for hours and found nothing.'

'Call off your officers. I'm close to solving this case. Please don't waste more police time on this futile exercise.'

Carp looked whipped. He was at a loss. 'I felt sure she'd hidden the weapon inside the house.' He checked his wristwatch. 'I'll give them another fifteen minutes and then we'll call it a day.'

'As you wish,' Fleming said. He was about to perch on the low garden wall when there was a shout.

'I've got something,' called a young constable atop a ladder inspecting the cottage roof.

'I knew it,' Carp said.

Carp and Fleming waited with bated breath as they stood at the foot of the constable's ladder.

The young officer put his hand as far down the gutter down-pipe as he could reach. 'I've nearly got it, sir.'

'The crafty old lady must have thought we'd never look there.'

Fleming said nothing.

'Be careful, son. Don't lose it,' Inspector Carp instructed.

The young constable closed his eyes and squeezed his hand down a little further. He stretched his fingers as far as they'd go. 'Got it!' He began bringing out his hand and wrist, which had almost got stuck. With the tips of his fingers, he pulled. 'It's feels like material, sir.'

Other officers gathered to witness what was about to be revealed.

'Nearly there, sir.' The constable pulled out the wet and slimy object and laid it on the roof tiles in front of him.

'Is it the weapon wrapped in material?' Carp yelled up to him. 'For goodness' sake, lad, what have you got?'

Red faced, the young constable turned his body at the top of the ladder. He held out the damp material. 'It's not the weapon, sir. It's a ladies' hat. It must have blown up here in a storm and got washed down the pipe.'

The other constables fell about laughing.

Carp wasn't amused. 'All right, you lot. Pack it in and pack it up, we're calling it a day. And you, son.' He pointed at the constable up the ladder. 'Get down here now. I want to have a word with you sharpish.' He turned to Fleming. 'It appears you're right about the dagger. However, the fact remains that Lily was the last person to see Valerie alive. In my book, that makes her my prime suspect in this investigation.'

CHAPTER ELEVEN

With so much on his mind, Fleming had decided to take a walk through the village. He'd reached the church and went inside to once again examine the crime scene.

The church was a modest size. Inside, the temperature was cool and the light low. Where the sun reached the stained glass windows, they dazzled. On either side of the centre aisle, two short rows of pews sat empty. Dead ahead of the aisle stood the altar, and behind that on the back wall was an old oak door to the vestry.

Over to the left, facing the pews, stood the pulpit. Fleming approached the altar where Valerie's body had lain. He moved quietly through the church, observing the stone carvings on pillars and plaques on the walls. The plaques were dedicated to those villagers who had fallen in battle or had been dignitaries.

Having circled around, he once again stood where Valerie had been so savagely attacked. Fleming took a seat close to the steps where she had fallen. He removed the precious ornate tin he kept in his jacket pocket and took out a piece of candied peel that had been prepared for him by Mrs Clayton. He sucked on the sweet treat as he looked around and pondered, trying to imagine what Valerie might have observed.

Footsteps from behind caused Fleming to turn. The vicar had arrived through the main doors. 'I'm sorry to have disturbed you. Please continue,' he said in a low voice.

'I was merely looking for inspiration.'

'The divine kind of inspiration?'

'Any kind,' Fleming admitted.

The vicar smiled. 'Whether I need to or not, I come here every day. My questions, and occasionally my prayers, are answered here. Are you a religious man, Henry?'

'My mother, who was deeply religious, brought me up to believe. It seems that like my memories of her, my faith is always with me.'

The vicar nodded thoughtfully. 'I gather you're working the case. Is there anything I can do to assist?'

'If you wouldn't mind?'

'It would be an honour.'

'In that case, would you stand where Valerie was attacked?' Fleming asked.

'Of course,' the vicar said. 'Just here?'

'Perfect. If I pretend to be the attacker, then I would want to approach without being noticed. The act of surprise gives me the advantage, and it means there would be no risk of struggle.'

'Ghastly,' the vicar said.

'Unfortunately, it's the truth.' Fleming moved around the vicar. The pews made it impossible to approach from the side without being noticed. Had they come from the front door and approached up the aisle, then it would have given Valerie time to flee to the vestry or call for help – assuming she was aware of the attacker's intention.

'That means the killer came from behind the altar and there's nothing there except the vestry.'

'On the night of the murder, I noticed a door inside the vestry. May I take another look?'

'Of course.' The vicar led the way and opened the door. It was a small room with a sink, a cupboard, a changing area, an armchair, and little more. 'This is the door. It's locked most of the time.' He reached up to a hook and took down a large iron key.

Fleming put out his hand for the key. 'May I?' He slipped the key into the lock and turned it. There was a *clunk* as the heavy locking mechanism shifted. He unfastened a bolt at the top of the door and another at the foot. With the old oak door open, he stepped out onto a patch of green where the grass was long and in need of mowing. Fleming took a few paces, then turned and looked back towards the waiting vicar. Where he had walked, the long grass had flattened. 'Our killer didn't enter or exit the church this way.'

'How can you be certain?'

'They would have flattened the grass like so.' He pointed to where he had walked.

'Of course.'

'The door interests me,' Fleming said. He returned to the vestry.

'In what way?'

Fleming ran a hand over the inside of the large wooden door.

'Unless the bolts had been left unfastened ahead of time, Valerie's killer wouldn't have been able to enter the church that way at the time of the murder.'

'They would have also needed a key.'

'On the night of the murder, I noticed the bolts were in place, which means it would have been impossible to exit that way. No, no. It is far too complicated and risky to have planned to come this way. Even if the door had been left unlocked by the killer ahead of the murder, they would be aware that either yourself or Valerie Toussaint might have noticed and relocked it.'

Inside the church, Fleming heard the sound of running footsteps. He hastily ran to the sound and was greeted by a panicked and panting Dicky Longbottom. 'You need to come quickly, Fleming. The vicar's wife has been attacked!'

The vicar appeared behind Fleming. 'What's that?'

'It's Barbara, she's hurt. A man attacked her.'

The three men rushed to the vicarage.

∿

BARBARA SAT on the edge of an armchair and held a bandage to her shoulder. She winced and gritted her teeth.

'This will steady your nerves,' Petunia said as she handed her a glass of brandy, then pulled Barbara's floral tunic aside to check and change the blood-soaked bandage. 'You're going to need stitches.'

'I'll drive you,' the vicar said.

'Thank goodness you're here,' Petunia said.

'Tell me what happened?' The vicar knelt in front of his wife.

'Give me a moment to calm myself.' Barbara drank the glass of brandy. Petunia refilled it then poured one for herself. 'I heard a noise outside. I thought you'd returned from the church. When you didn't appear, I went to the front door and called out. When I got no reply, I stepped outside, and that's when I was grabbed and felt a thump. I fought him off and managed to get back in the house. It wasn't until I was safely inside that I realised the thump I'd felt was actually where I'd been cut.'

'You were stabbed,' Petunia corrected. She lifted the bandage to reveal a puncture wound.

'It's nothing,' Barbara said. 'A scrape.'

'It looks far worse than that,' Dicky said.

'Did you get a look at your attacker?' Fleming asked.

'Not really. It all happened so fast.'

'How about yourselves?' he asked Petunia and Dicky.

'We were passing only moments after it happened but saw nobody,' Petunia said.

Fleming turned to Barbara. 'You said it was a man. How can you be sure?'

'He was strong. Big hands. Tall.'

'Did he say anything?'

Barbara shuddered. 'When he spoke, he almost growled. He said "It was meant to be you."'

'It was meant to be you?' the vicar repeated. He began trembling. 'I could have lost you.'

'What do you think he meant by that?' Petunia asked.

'It's obvious,' the vicar said. 'The killer hadn't

meant to murder Valerie. His intended target had been Barbara all along.'

'This changes everything,' Dicky said. 'For one thing, it'll clear Lily.'

'I don't think Inspector Carp will see it that way. It's very likely he'll see the two attacks as unrelated.'

'But the attacker said, "It was meant to be you". Surely that can mean only one thing,' Petunia insisted.

'Unfortunately, despite what we may think, it could mean many things.'

'There's something else,' Barbara said. She reached into her pocket and pulled out a folded piece of paper and an envelope. She handed them to Fleming. He took the paper and examined it closely. Having read it, he turned it around in his hands, sniffed it, and held it up to the light. He did the same to the envelope.

'When it arrived, I thought it was a joke. Someone's idea of fun. You know, scare the vicar's wife. Children perhaps. They can be wicked and thoughtless.'

'What is it?' the vicar asked.

Fleming handed it to him. 'A threat.'

'What does it say?' Petunia asked.

The words were formed using letters cut from a newspaper and stuck to cream writing paper.

I WILL KILL YOU FOR WHAT YOU'VE DONE

The vicar's eyes widened. 'When did you get this? Why didn't you tell me?'

'It came this morning. You have enough on your plate. I didn't want to trouble you. As I said, I thought it was a foolish bit of fun sent by some of the school-children.'

'It's far from a childish joke,' Fleming insisted.

'Kill you for what?' Dicky asked. 'What have you ever done to anyone?'

'I don't know,' Barbara said. 'It's clearly someone who's deranged.'

'What do we do now?' the vicar asked. 'We need police help.'

'Take Barbara to see a doctor and inform Inspector Carp. He must see this note and take a statement.'

'What will you do?' Barbara asked.

'I'll continue to examine the facts and then carefully consider everything I've learned. This case is more complex than I first thought.'

In the event though, Fleming insisted on driving Barbara and the vicar to the hospital. Once there, he spoke privately and at length to the doctor about the shoulder wound.

When Inspector Carp arrived, Fleming was invited to listen once again to Barbara's story of the terrifying attack.

'What do you make of it all?' Inspector Carp asked

when the interview was over. 'Do you think it's related to Valerie Toussaint's murder?'

'The regrettable fact is, Inspector, this case has frustrated me from start to finish. I think I'm getting close to a solution when...' He raised his hands in exasperation. 'One thing is apparent, and it's something I'm ashamed to admit. I've allowed my friendship with Lily to cloud my thinking. To solve this case, I must remove my own personal emotions. I need to get away. Escape Fulbridge. I must allow myself the freedom to examine this puzzle from afar.'

'You're leaving?' Inspector Carp looked shocked.

'For a day or two. No more. When I return, I'll know what to do. There's one person I must speak to before I depart.'

~

ON THE OUTSKIRTS of the village, Warren Silvers stood on the old wooden bridge, after which the village was named, and watched the sun climb. Where the warmth of the sun touched the cool fields, a mist rose into the air. Beneath his feet, the river gurgled along. In the last few days, the morning chorus had lost its usual beauty. He'd once enjoyed rising before the rest of the world and having this part of the day to himself. It was as if he got to experience a moment of creation. A sacred and secret time that felt as if it belonged to him, and him alone. Today, that feeling eluded him.

The bridge creaked as Fleming stepped onto it.

Warren turned to face him. He spoke in a low voice. 'Good morning.'

'Good morning. It's a beautiful one, to be sure.'

Fleming joined Warren in admiring the sunrise. 'Did you know Aboriginal Australians say that long, long ago, there was no light?' Fleming asked. 'They say that animals were fed up with the cold and black, where they would bump into one another, and were unable to find food for days at a time. They say the birds called a meeting for all the animals and it was decided the magpies would raise the sky by gathering sticks and pushing the sky up. Which they did with great effort. Now, every morning, the Sun-Woman rises in the east and carries a fiery torch across the sky. That's why, overjoyed by the sun's warmth and beauty, the birds greet each day with a wonderful song.'

Warren grinned. 'Is that a genuine story?'

Fleming nodded. 'I paraphrased a little.'

'Is Barbara all right?' Warren asked. 'I heard what happened.'

'Shocked from the attack. Physically, she'll be okay.'

'I'll take her some flowers later.'

'She'll like that.'

'You can stop the small talk. I'm sure you didn't get up so early to catch me alone to tell me your story.'

Fleming smiled. 'I don't have a question. It's more a favour.'

'A favour?'

'There are some errands I need to attend to and so I must leave for a couple of days. I wondered if you'd feed Kitty.'

'Of course. Anything else?'

Fleming's eyes appraised him. 'In a day or two, I would like to call upon you to create a distraction. I intend to put on a show to reveal what really happened to Valerie. Would you do that for me?'

Warren sighed and turned back to the dawn. 'This is it? The truth is finally coming out? It'll be a relief when it's finally over.'

Fleming slowly walked away.

CHAPTER TWELVE

TWO DAYS LATER

Lily Riley sat beside Inspector Carp in the left front row of the church. Facing forward, she kept her eyes fixed on the large stained-glass window ahead of her. She didn't look around, or allow her focus to deviate, as the other villagers arrived. With the help of Inspector Carp, Fleming had arranged for key members of the village to be assembled at the scene of the crime.

As they arrived, a magnificent bouquet of yellow roses drew everyone's eye to the church altar.

The vicar and his wife were the first, and chose the pew behind Lily. Barbara put a comforting hand on Lily's shoulder and whispered her support. Lily still did not look back. Instead, she whispered over her shoulder, 'Thank you.'

Olivia and Keith Bennett followed. Without a word to one another, or anyone else gathered, they went to their usual Sunday service seats in the second row on the right-hand side, away from the aisle. The front row on the right side remained empty.

Petunia Longbottom chose her aisle seat on the right in the third row. She smiled and nodded to the vicar and Barbara. Keith turned and greeted her. Olivia had bowed her head in prayer and did not look up.

A few minutes later, Dicky Longbottom sent everyone's heart racing as he stumbled through the church doors, disturbing the quiet and causing an almighty clatter. 'Sorry. Apologies,' he whispered to all. 'I knew I shouldn't have worn my clown shoes today.' He chuckled alone. Taking a seat beside Petunia, he tried desperately not to giggle. 'This is all very odd. Where's Fleming?'

'Sh!' Petunia said.

'Well, where is he?' he whispered.

Warren Silvers came in next. He was dressed in a black suit with a lime green shirt. His neck-tie was red and held in place with a gold tie-clip. He chose the aisle seat behind everyone else in the third row to the left.

Dicky looked across at Warren, but Warren wouldn't catch his eye.

With Inspector Carp and all eight villagers now arrived, Fleming made his entrance. Without a word or glance to any of the assembled, he marched to the front of the church. All heads raised, and all eyes fixed on him. In his brown tweed three-piece suit and exuding certainty and composure, he commanded everyone's attention.

'I would like to thank you all for coming today and especially Inspector Carp, for his patience with me. I'm aware I've been something of an irritation. Something I hear regularly when involved in an investigation.' He held up a hand to prevent his refuting the fact. 'My methods are occasionally unorthodox, as I'm no longer bound by the constraints of usual police procedure. This, however, offers me freedom of mind and accords me the opportunity to explore possibilities not always afforded officers of the law. Today's experiment is a case in point.'

Inspector Carp cleared his throat and shifted uncomfortably. 'It seems you have friends in high places, Fleming. Today's – whatever this is – has been granted by those well above my pay grade. I can't say I entirely agree with what's about to take place, but I'll go along for the ride as instructed.'

Fleming nodded his gratitude.

'He makes a good point, Mr Fleming. What *is* this all about?' Olivia Bennett asked.

'It's all quite simple. I plan to reveal Valerie Toussaint's murderer. I will explain why she was murdered and, finally, how it was done.'

A low murmur filled the church as the gathered group could hardly believe their ears.

Lily didn't flinch. Her eyes remained focused on the stained-glass window ahead of her.

'So who was it?' Barbara asked. 'I don't feel entirely comfortable knowing the person who murdered Valerie and attacked me is now only a few feet away.' Her accusing eyes leapt from person to person.

'All in good time. You're perfectly safe. I've asked Inspector Carp to station police constables outside for everyone's safety.'

'That order came from the very top,' Carp grunted. 'Like I said, Fleming has friends in high places. Seeing as you got us all here, can we assume you know who the killer is?'

'I know exactly who did it. The only question that remains is where to begin?' Fleming mused. 'There is no denying Valerie Toussaint was a complicated woman who was liked and disliked in equal measure. To some, she was a close friend. To others, her beauty, both inside and out, was a fascination. Others found her an irritation. While at least one person here despised her enough to commit the most heinous act. Ultimately ending in her life being cut tragically short.'

Warren could not control a sob that he'd been holding onto. He clenched his hands tight in his lap.

Olivia Bennett dabbed her nose with a handkerchief while, next to her, Keith Bennett shifted uneasily in his seat.

Fleming walked down the aisle and back up again, all eyes following him. 'Lily Riley has been accused of killing her friend Valerie Toussaint. The only motive put forward is that of money. The new venture she had with Valerie, bringing their jam to the masses with Lily's face, reputation and household name, as the brand. Cashing in on her celebrity as an author to promote the quintessentially English produce.'

Carp spoke up. 'Lily and Valerie stood to gain a small fortune from the deal and, with Valerie out of the way, Lily can pocket the lot. Makes perfect sense she killed her.'

'It would, Inspector. However, Lily has no interest in fame or additional wealth. She retreated from it all to live a simple life with her late husband, William. Over the years, she's been offered numerous lucrative book deals, and each time she's turned them down. She has money. More than she will ever need. With no children as heirs, what need has she of money? None, is the answer. Her life out of the spotlight is comfortable.'

'Her face on every label will surely put her back in the spotlight,' Barbara suggested.

'You are correct. I pondered this for quite some time. Then, I learned that as part of the deal, she herself would do no publicity work. None. Her name and image would be used with her permission and only because of her status as a well-known novelist. It was her *name* that the company wanted, not *her*. She could continue to live her very private life away from the glare of fame.'

'The money?' Barbara asked.

'As part of the deal, she receives very little. The majority will go to charity and good causes.'

There was more low murmuring.

'It's the charities that benefit, not Lily herself. You see, Lily Riley doesn't stand to benefit from Valerie's death. In fact, she actively sought to reject the business proposal. It was only because of Valerie's own financial distress, and her suggestion of the good that could come from her involvement, that Lily finally capitulated, and agreed.'

'If there's no motive, then how can the police have charged Lily with the murder?' Petunia asked.

'To charge someone with a criminal offence, the motive isn't required,' Carp explained. 'Though it's helpful when attempting to prove guilt in court,' he admitted.

'What about a murder weapon?' Dicky added.

'We believe Lily's missing dagger was used,' Carp insisted.

'Yet, you haven't actually found the weapon?'

Carp tugged at his shirt collar. 'We're working on it. It'll turn up.'

'It all sounds rather flimsy to me,' Dicky muttered privately to his wife.

Fleming raised his hands to silence the rumblings of concern. 'With no clear motive nailed down, the next question is why, then, is Lily the prime suspect? The answer is simple. She had the opportunity. She was the last known person with Valerie before she died.'

Carp nodded enthusiastically. 'Exactly. There's no point in overcomplicating matters. It can't have been anyone else.'

'If you're saying it wasn't Lily, then who was it?' Petunia asked.

'All in good time,' Fleming said. 'Since you're keen to hear the truth, let's start with you.'

'Me? I had nothing to do with it.' Petunia's face became thunderous. She looked at her husband for support.

'You can't think either of us is involved, Fleming. That's absurd,' Dicky blustered. He clasped his wife's hand.

'If I may be so indelicate, it's well known that Petunia has a temper. Which at times she finds difficult to control. I was made aware of this on the day of the village fete, when she discovered her jam jar labels ruined by water damage, in a fit of anger she took out her frustration on her friend Warren. She was also furious with judge Valerie and, full of resentment, she went to her home and destroyed two pieces of prized topiary sculptures in her garden.'

Petunia jumped to her feet. 'That's something I'm not proud of! I should have conducted myself better. I'll be the first to admit I'm a handful at times. My frustrations get the better of me, but that does *not* make me a murderer.'

'She's right,' Dicky said. He, too, got to his feet. 'I'll not put up with this.'

Fleming raised a soothing hand. 'You are the devoted husband, Dicky. You would give your darling wife whatever she desires. You see her outbursts for what they are. You alone understand and forgive her tirades. She's shared with you why such anger is harboured inside.'

'Now listen here, Fleming. If you're about to suggest I murdered Valerie on Petunia's behalf, then you have it all wrong.'

'On the contrary. You're a gentleman. A little rough around the edges perhaps, but a forgiving and caring soulmate. It's Petunia's fear of losing you that contributes to her outbursts. I only had to do a little digging to discover Petunia's abandonment by her mother. A little girl who's wondered her whole life why her mother didn't want her, and whether she'd done something wrong for her mother to give her up. It's a tragic and heavy burden she carries in her heart.'

Petunia's face softened. Fleming gave her the time she needed to explain herself.

'After she passed away, I received a letter from my mother,' Petunia explained. 'In the letter, she expressed her many regrets. How not a day had passed that she didn't wish things had been different. She explained how she suffered her whole life with a malady that left her bedridden for weeks, and months, at a time. As a young mother, she could barely look after herself, let alone a child. When my father lost his life, she felt she had no choice but to give me up. An opportunity presented itself when she spoke to a childless couple living nearby. Together, they decided it would be best if I wasn't told the truth. Growing up, I knew they weren't my parents, and I called them uncle and auntie. They loved me like their own. I loved them. Yet, as a child, I invented many reasons why my mother abandoned me. Some were good and some bad. What really hurt was that after her death, I discovered she'd lived only minutes away from where I grew up. I could have helped her. I could have shown her love. She could have loved me.' Tears forced their way to the surface. Dicky wrapped an arm around her.

'This is why you want to get away from this village. You want to return to London and be close to where you grew up and, most importantly, where your mother had lived.'

'I need to find the connection that I never had. I can't do that in this place. I never had anything against Valerie. I was jealous, perhaps. Her life seemed so perfect and together and it annoyed me. However, I thought, in time, we might have been friends. We'll never know.'

Fleming turned to Warren Silvers.

CHAPTER THIRTEEN

'You, Warren Silvers, are what might be called a long-suffering friend of Petunia.'

He grinned and winked at her. 'That I am. Deep down, she has a heart of gold. We're kindred spirits.'

'Why do you think you bonded with Petunia?'

'I recognised our affinity immediately. I too have had a lot of pain in my life. You see, I'm different from most everyone else. I don't conform. I wear what I like, make friends of my choosing, and live the way I want to. People don't always like that. I see Petunia as the sister I never had, but always wanted.'

'Do you think Petunia opened up to you about her childhood because of your bond?'

'Yes. I'm also a good listener, so I'm told.'

'I see.' Fleming walked to where Warren was seated. 'You're also an incredibly talented artist.'

'I don't like to blow my own trumpet, but I'm quite good.'

'Such modesty. Despite your success, I learned you no longer exhibit your extraordinary art in major cities.'

'I prefer exclusivity. Exhibiting means critics. I don't take criticism well. A judge's tongue can be a cruel lash.'

'You sell your work to private buyers?'

'I eke out a living. I'm not bitter. I prefer it this way. People move to small towns for lots of reasons. Despite this flamboyant persona, I'm the shy type.' He chuckled. 'I also shun confrontation.'

'This is true. It makes one wonder though, how far you'd actually go to avoid confrontation.'

Warren's smile faltered 'I hardly *avoid* it. If that were the case, I'd avoid Petunia like the plague!' He laughed and blew her a kiss.

'You were also friends with Valerie.'

'I try to be friends with everyone.' He chuckled nervously. 'I like to please people. It brings me joy. Friends, art, and champagne. The perfect combination for a happy life. Though not necessarily in that order.' He laughed.

'And you enjoy walking, especially wide open spaces?'

'I love walking. Early mornings and late evenings.

It provides inspiration, and that's like oxygen for an artist.'

'Would you say you have a keen eye? Being an artist, and taking in the world around you?'

'Definitely.'

'It was when you were returning from one of your walks on the evening of the murder that you saw someone other than Lily enter the church.'

'There was someone else?' the vicar asked.

Warren looked around at all the faces staring at him and was suddenly lost for words. 'I saw Petunia and Dicky out for a walk, but only from a distance. We didn't stop and speak.' He smiled weakly.

Fleming looked encouragingly at Warren. 'I need you to explain to everyone who else you saw. I know you're being forced to keep it secret but, for Lily's sake, and in Valerie's memory, it's time to be truthful.' He placed a supportive hand on his shoulder and whispered in his ear. 'You can do this. Tell everyone what you told me.'

Warren took a deep breath and summoned his courage. 'I did see someone. I'd been for a walk to the river. It was only a short walk because I'd been left tired after the excitement of the fete.'

Fleming became more insistent. 'Who did you see?'

'I saw Keith Bennett enter the church,' Warren blurted. 'He waited for Lily to come out.'

'Utter nonsense!' Olivia Bennett interrupted. 'He's a liar. You can't trust a word this man says.'

Warren lowered his head. 'I saw Lily come out of the church, then Keith go in.'

'Speak up, please,' Fleming said.

'I sat on a bench near the church because I'd had a lovely day and didn't want it to end. I was still revelling in my win at the fete. I was listening to the birds and enjoying the evening air. As I sat there, I watched as Lily came out of the church. She looked distracted. She started walking towards her cottage. I then noticed Keith Bennett. He was watching Lily and waiting. In his hand he had a bouquet of roses.'

'Did Lily see him go in?'

'No.'

'You're a liar!' Olivia yelled again.

'You know it's the truth,' Warren said. 'That's why you forced me not to tell the police.'

'She forced you?' Fleming asked in a way that made it clear he already knew the answer.

'Olivia discovered my secret and threatened to tell the village I was a fraud. She wanted to tell everyone I'm a criminal and promised to ruin my life.'

'That's not true. What it does do, though, is prove you can't be trusted. That you lie and cheat.'

Warren jumped to his feet. 'I forged a painting and

tried to sell it. There! Now the whole village will know! Happy now?'

'Finally, some truth,' Olivia yelled.

'I was caught, and I went to prison. I was young. A penniless student. I was foolish. I thought I could make some quick money. It's also the real reason I work here in the village. It's better for sales if I remain anonymous. When I achieved success in my own right, my dubious background hit the papers. My name and face are well known in the art world. Olivia must have come across an old article, I presume.'

'You served your time,' Fleming observed.

'Yes. I learned my lesson. Everything I've created since is my own.' He slumped back down in his seat.

'You were young and naïve and you paid the price. You learned from it,' Fleming said. 'Many would say you deserve a second chance.'

'I had hoped so. I suppose only time will tell.'

Fleming nodded in gratitude to Warren. 'Thank you for your bravery here today.' He then turned to Keith, who'd flushed pink. Beads of sweat had formed on his face and neck.

'I went to see her,' he exclaimed. 'Valerie, I mean.'

Olivia scowled. 'Don't say a word, you fool. You'll get yourself locked up.'

'I already know the truth, Keith,' Fleming said. 'It's

better you tell us in your own words. However, if you prefer, I'll be happy to oblige on your behalf.'

'It's none of your business,' Olivia said. She clasped her hands and wrung them furiously. 'I don't know who you think you are to humiliate people in this way?'

'It's okay,' Keith said. 'It's time to get everything out in the open. Let's stop pretending.'

'I don't want you to tell them,' Olivia sobbed. 'It's our business. Nobody else's.'

'I'm tired of the lies and secrecy, Livvy. It's exhausting.'

'I can't lose you.'

'It's okay. I won't ever leave you.' He kissed Olivia on the forehead. Keith got to his feet and turned to look at everyone. 'I was in love with Valerie. It was ridiculous, I know. Olivia told me I was a fool. I knew Valerie was out of my league. She was right. Yet, I couldn't help myself. I couldn't stop thinking about her. When she spoke to me, my mouth went dry, my heart raced like a locomotive, and I became tongue-tied like a silly teenager. It was the first time in my life I'd ever felt this way.'

Barbara Ardern frowned. 'I don't understand. How can you stand there and say that in front of your wife? Olivia must feel crushed?'

'He knows!' exclaimed Keith, pointing at Fleming. 'Why don't you tell them?'

Fleming returned to the front of the church and faced those gathered. 'The answer's simple. They're not husband and wife. They have never married.'

'What are you saying?' Barbara asked. 'I'm confused.'

'Olivia and Keith are not, and have never been, husband and wife. They are brother and sister.'

'Keith is my brother.' Olivia got to her feet. 'It's all very simple. We decided a few years ago that it was easier to pretend we were married than to keep answering questions about why an unmarried brother and sister lived together. I realised long ago I didn't want to marry. Keith had given up on ever finding love, so it was easier this way. I put on my mother's wedding ring when she passed away, and we hatched the plan. No more unsolicited questions, or speculation, or horrid whispers about why there was no *Mr Right*. After a few years, Keith and I promised we'd be there for each other in old age. I know it sounds selfish, but having my big brother around gives me security. We look out for each other. That's what I was doing when I realised he had feelings for Valerie, looking out for him.'

'I'll always be there for you, Olivia. I simply fell in

love with the idea of Valerie and myself being together. I now realise it was a fantasy.'

'Olivia lied to me when she told me you'd confessed your love for her months ago. In fact, it was the evening of the fete that you opened up to her about your feelings.'

Keith nodded. 'Quite true.'

'You took her flowers. Yellow roses. I discovered a yellow rose petal in her hand,' Fleming said.

'I did. As she does every Saturday evening, Valerie was preparing the church for Sunday service. I'd finally plucked up enough courage to tell her how I felt.'

'Yet, she didn't respond in a way you'd hoped. In fact, she rejected you,' Fleming stated.

'It's fair to say it was the most humiliating moment of my life. I expressed my love for her and she thought I was joking. She laughed. When she realised I was serious, the damage was done. Patronisingly, she informed me I was adorable, but not in the way she could ever consider romantic.'

Olivia put a hand on her brother's arm to comfort him. 'I'm sorry.'

Keith swallowed hard and continued. 'I felt crushed. My embarrassment turned to anger. I called her a heartless tease and stormed out of the church. The last thing I ever said to her was out of spite.' His bottom lip trembled as he fought his emotions.

'When you left her, she was alone?'

'Yes. I rushed out and went home. Like a child, I ran to my bedroom and locked the door and wouldn't come out. In fact, I didn't come out until I heard there had been an incident at the church.'

Fleming pressed Keith for the truth. 'You expect us to believe that you didn't harm her? You were the last person to see her alive. The truth is, she humiliated you and you attacked her. You stabbed her in the heart?'

Keith's body began to tremble. 'That's not what happened.'

Fleming pressed him harder. 'Your actions are those of a guilty man. You saw Warren as you left the church and told Olivia, making her your accomplice when she threatened Warren to ensure his silence.'

Keith shook his head. His mouth opened and shut. He had no words.

'You pretended you had no feelings for Valerie. A charade for all of us here. You also kept from the police you had seen her right before her death. Allowing Lily to take the blame. You have behaved despicably. Yours are the actions of a man who has something to hide.'

'It wasn't Keith who killed her,' Olivia yelled. 'He wouldn't have harmed a hair on her head.'

Keith pulled himself together. 'I was aware of how it would look. She had rejected me right before her death. The police would assume the worst.'

'We'd have conducted a full and thorough investigation, is what we would have done,' Carp replied.

'Indeed,' Fleming said. 'It's my belief that Lily was on her way home from the church when she went back to make amends with Valerie. She could not have slept well, knowing their argument was unresolved.'

'In the fading light, she didn't see you dashing away carrying the bouquet of roses.' Fleming turned to Lily. She had finally stopped looking straight ahead. She looked at Fleming, who now faced her. 'Lily returned to the church to make amends with her friend, only to find her brutally murdered. It would, therefore, seem obvious to most that it was in fact Keith, and not Lily, who, in a fit of despair, murdered his beloved Valerie. After all, he's a shy man, humiliated, and left with an irreparably broken heart.'

'I'll admit to being a broken-hearted fool. Of that, there's no doubt. But I'm not a killer!' Keith insisted.

'No. You're not the killer,' Fleming pronounced. 'That despicable crime belongs to someone else.' Fleming's steely focus turned to the vicar.

CHAPTER FOURTEEN

'Y ou've gone mad, Fleming,' Dicky announced. 'I simply won't believe it was Jonathan! A vicar wouldn't do such a thing.'

Fleming moved close to the vicar and his wife as he addressed them all. 'I've examined many cases over the years and of one thing, I'm certain. Men and women, no matter their profession, or background, under the right circumstances, are certainly capable of murder.'

The vicar's face had turned ashen. His mouth moved, but no sound came out. He stared hard at Fleming.

Fleming stared back at him. 'We both know it wasn't you that killed Valerie, don't we?' Fleming said.

The vicar looked momentarily confused. Then his eyes widened. He turned his head slowly. He looked at everyone gathered until his eyes finally came to rest on his wife. 'Was it you?' he asked.

Barbara shook her head. 'I was fast asleep when it happened. I was in bed. Remember?'

The vicar slumped back in his seat. He saw something in his wife's face that convinced him she was lying. 'What have you done?'

Fleming took over again. 'At first, it seems impossible for you to have been in two places at once. In my mind, I thought it inconceivable that you could have come to the church unseen by either Lily or Keith and killed Valerie Toussaint as she tended your husband's church. I, too, preferred the obvious solution that one of these two had indeed committed the crime. However, neither option was easy to comprehend. I considered many other options and suspects. One by one, I eliminated the others until only one remained. I then merely had to consider how I would have done it, if I were you and didn't want to risk being seen or caught in the act. It was only when I accidentally stumbled upon a magician's props that the answer came to me in a flash!'

Barbara took her husband's hand. 'He's talking nonsense, dear. How could I possibly get from the vicarage to the church unseen? We should leave. We've heard enough of this stuff and nonsense.'

'It's I who's heard enough. Enough of your lies!

You will remain seated and allow me to demonstrate.' Fleming stepped away from the altar. He marched down the aisle and out of the church.

'He's gone?' Warren got to his feet and went to the front of the church where Fleming had been standing. 'I was asked before the meeting today to make sure everyone remains seated; no matter what happens, nobody is to leave.'

'You're in on this absurdity?' Barbara asked.

'I don't understand,' Petunia said.

'Is he coming back?' Olivia wondered.

'Everyone remain calm,' Carp insisted. He was clearly as bemused as everyone else, but keen nobody left while he assessed the situation. 'I think we should wait here like Mr Silvers suggests. Fleming might be fetching something to aid him in his theatrics. Let's give him a few minutes.'

The gathered began chatting amongst themselves. Some ten minutes later, a nervous Warren suggested Dicky take a look outside without leaving the church.

Everyone nodded in agreement. 'Yes, take a look.'

Dicky walked tentatively to the church doors.

All eyes were on him as he peered outside.

Suddenly there was a shriek from Lily.

All heads turned back to the front of the church.

Fleming had reappeared at the altar, standing behind Warren.

He had miraculously re-entered the church without being seen. Somehow he'd neither come through the front door, nor the vestry door, which remained shut.

'I apologise if my demonstration alarmed you,' Fleming said.

Lily put a calming hand to her heart.

Fleming pressed on. 'As you can see, Warren was completely unaware of my approach. As Valerie would have been at Barbara's advance on the night of her death. Her mind was no doubt contemplating her recent entanglement with Keith. She then bent down to pick up the dropped rose petal I found in her hand. As she turned back towards the altar, Barbara Ardern struck her with a fatal blow using the dagger taken from Lily's cottage.'

Barbara shook her head. 'Absurd.'

'How did you, and she, get in to the church unseen?' Lily asked.

'A priest's hole. A hidden chamber leading to a tunnel beneath the church. Most likely created during the sixteenth century when Catholic priests were lawfully persecuted by the Crown. It was Inspector Carp who brought it to my attention when he unsuccessfully searched Lily's cottage for the murder weapon.'

Everyone got to their feet and examined the hideaway. A square, hinged, tiled section of the floor behind the altar had been lifted. Peering inside, there were steps leading to a cramped space where the priest could hide from the Queen's soldiers.

'Below is where I stayed overnight when I claimed to have gone to London,' Fleming said. 'Wrapped in a blanket, I slept through the cold night and emerged late the next day unobserved.'

'Surely the vicar would have noticed Barbara missing from the vicarage?' Olivia suggested.

'Having claimed to be suffering from a migraine, Barbara waited until the vicar had gone to pray with a sick parishioner at the hospital. She then slipped through the entrance of the tunnel in the vicarage. There's a wooden panel beside the fireplace, which I discovered after following the tunnel from this entrance. Inside the tunnel, she crept until finally she emerged in the church completely unnoticed. She then hid and awaited her opportunity. Having watched Keith and Valerie's interaction, she waited for him to leave. Barbara then took her chance and killed Valerie in cold blood. Then, returning along the tunnel and back to her room, she resumed her charade of requiring an early night.'

'Utter twaddle,' Barbara exclaimed. She slowly clapped her hands as though applauding his far-fetched nonsense. 'And if any of it were true, which it isn't, where's your proof?'

'You left a trace of Valerie's blood on the inside of the priest's hole as you climbed down the steps.'

'Anybody could have left a smear of her blood. It doesn't mean it was me.'

'Not just anybody,' Fleming explained. 'The tunnel leads directly to your home, the vicarage. I also found a fabric thread that, upon examination, will match your clothing. I suspect a pair of black trousers. There's also the fact that the timing of the murder coincided with your husband's absence, giving you the opportunity.'

'It sounds to me like you're clutching at straws. I'm the wife of a village vicar. Not a murderer.'

Fleming's eyes narrowed. 'I also found the murder weapon.'

'You have it?!' Carp exclaimed.

'I spent most of my time while in the tunnel searching for it. I felt sure the killer would have hidden it there. When it's examined, your fingerprints will be on it and so will Valerie Toussaint's blood. That's the evidence.'

'What of the threatening letter that she was sent?' Carp asked.

'Fabricated by Barbara to once again throw me off the scent.'

'Are you suggesting she stabbed herself? Made up the story of being attacked?' the vicar asked.

'Most definitely,' Fleming insisted.

'But why?' the vicar asked, turning to his wife.

Barbara returned to the front row of the pews and sat down. She didn't appear defeated or repentant. 'The reason I did it doesn't matter now.'

'It's important you explain,' her husband said. 'I have to understand.' He was on one knee in front of her, holding her hands.

'Valerie refused to allow me to be a part of the business venture.'

'What business venture? Is this to do with the jam?' The vicar's eyes widened.

'I deserved to be part of it. The traditional village fete, and the chance to show produce, was something I worked on tirelessly here in Fulbridge. I helped them get their jams into local shops, then city shops. They wouldn't even have been noticed by investors if I hadn't played my part, but Valerie refused to acknowledge my contribution. The business could have made us rich beyond our wildest dreams.'

'We don't need the money,' the vicar insisted. 'You know that. I'm not motivated by money.'

'Don't talk nonsense. You tell me all the time about how much good you could do, all the lives you could change for the better, if you only had more money.'

The vicar put his head in his hands. 'I don't believe this is happening.'

'Unfortunately, it's true,' Fleming said. 'The motive is money, and differences of opinion. Valerie left Barbara out of the deal. Barbara felt it was her contribution that started the ball rolling, and that ultimately Valerie stole from her. When they sold the rights to the brand, Barbara felt she was also entitled to a windfall. Over the years, it will equate to tens of thousands of pounds. Presumably, Valerie wouldn't listen to reason. So she went to Lily and asked her to persuade Valerie to make her an equal partner.'

Barbara looked indignant. 'I went to Lily's home and explained how I felt I'd been unjustly treated. I'd had the original idea for the traditional English jam company. I could see Lily's celebrity still had value. I'd mentioned putting Lily's face and name on the label because people consider her a national treasure. I pleaded my case, but she insisted she didn't want anything to do with the negotiations. That's when I took the dagger. When Lily left the room for a few minutes, I removed it from the box. I don't know what possessed me. I was angry with her. I just wanted to take something she loved. I knew she and Valerie both had a Cleopatra's dagger and so it seemed appropriate.'

'It also meant suspicion would then fall on Lily, and not yourself, after the murder.'

'At the time, that didn't occur to me. Only later, after I'd done it, did it work out to be advantageous. It meant they were both punished.'

'Yet, you planned the murder?' Fleming asked.

'I only intended to threaten her. Make her see sense. I tried asking nicely.'

'She wouldn't listen?'

Barbara shook her head. 'I decided to fake a headache so I could go to bed early. I also had a drink of wine, but not to excess. When Jonathan checked on me before visiting the hospital, everything appeared normal. I pretended to be sleeping. When I heard the front door close and I was sure he'd left, I entered the priest's hole and followed the tunnel to the church. I went that way so I wasn't seen.'

'I learned that some priest's holes are just that, a hole in the ground,' Fleming explained proudly. 'Others, like the one in this church, were attached to tunnels so the priest could escape. When I found the entrance here in the church, I realised I had the final piece of the puzzle. In years gone by, it had been a perfect bolt-hole for those evading persecution. More recently, it made an ideal escape route for a killer fleeing a murder scene.'

Barbara nodded. 'When I reached the church, I

found Valerie and Keith talking. I saw him offer the flowers. Keith then got angry and snatched them back. When he stormed off, she stooped down to pick up what I now know was the rose petal. When I came up behind her she jumped up and, with the shock of seeing me, she shoved me. She got really angry. She shoved me again. I pulled out the knife. I'd only brought it with me to threaten her. When she laughed in my face and mocked me, I... I stabbed her. I panicked. I ran back through the tunnel and hid the dagger along the way. Once I'd returned to my bed, I acted as if nothing had happened.'

'Unfortunately, the repercussions of your actions had far-reaching consequences.'

'As far as I can see, they brought it all upon themselves. They stole my idea and money due.'

'I'm sorry you see it that way,' Lily said. 'I think Valerie would have said there was no idea to be had. The buyers simply wanted my name attached to the jam. So you see, the argument could go round and round in circles forever.'

'You heard from Keith how cold-hearted Valerie could be. I no longer need to prove my case.'

Lily looked pitifully at Barbara. 'The reason Valerie and I argued that evening was because of you.'

'Really? About what?'

'As you requested, I went to her. I insisted you were

made an equal partner. At first, she refused. She wouldn't give up any of her share. I suggested you received part of my share. When she realised I wasn't going to back down, and that I was serious she changed her mind. She wanted no animosity among us. She agreed to split it three ways.'

'I don't believe you.'

'It's true. You killed her for no reason. You were to receive a full share.'

Barbara's indignation evaporated.

'The attack on you,' Fleming said. 'The shoulder wound you received. It was self-inflicted. Intended to allay my suspicions here in the village?'

'I thought you might look elsewhere for a suspect. I fabricated the whole mystery attacker. I cut myself with a kitchen knife. Then went outside and called for help.'

'I think we've heard enough,' Fleming said. 'A woman has lost her life in the most terrible way and it appears her killer shows no remorse. I hope in time this changes.'

'I agree,' Inspector Carp said. He called two constables and Barbara was led away. He then turned to Lily. 'My apologies, Mrs Riley. It appears my suspicions were misplaced. You are free to go.'

CHAPTER FIFTEEN

A week after Barbara's arrest, Fleming was driving through Fulbridge in his car. He had been helping Inspector Carp put together the case against Barbara and was travelling back to Lily's cottage. Outside the post office he passed the vicar on his bicycle. Their eyes met, and Fleming instinctively raised a hand in recognition. The vicar's gaze was steely and cold. He turned away, his face full of resentment as he pedalled on. It was a sad fact that the sentence that would soon be handed down to Barbara would be severe. It would also be harsh for those who had loved her.

~

'I'm ARTHUR,' Arthur Pudding said. 'Olivia's friend.'

Keith put out his hand. 'It's a pleasure to finally meet you, Mr Pudding. Olivia's told me a lot about you.'

Olivia looked nervously at Keith, and then adoringly at Arthur. 'I'll fetch us some drinks. I have fresh lemonade in the pantry.'

Keith and Arthur sat at the table that had been set up in the garden. It was a hot day. The table was beneath a silver birch which offered some shade from the sun.

Keith cleared his throat and chewed the inside of his mouth. He looked around to make sure Olivia wasn't in earshot before speaking. 'I'm not one for big speeches, though I do have a few things I need to get off my chest. I'll speak plainly, and I'll speak my mind. If you don't mind?'

Arthur nodded. 'Please do.'

'As you're no doubt aware, my Livvy, Olivia, gave up on ever falling in love. Also, marriage and all that entails. I hope she won't mind my saying, but she's no young girl any more. She's a woman and an older woman at that. That said, her heart is as fragile as any young girl's.' Keith cleared his throat again. 'What I'm trying to say is she's happy. I've never seen her as happy as she is when she's been around you, or is talking about you. She's my little sister. She might be all grown up, but she's still that same little girl inside. Full of hope and dreams. I want you to know that I couldn't be happier she found you.'

'That's very kind of you, Keith. I adore Olivia. In fact, I love her.'

'Don't break her heart.'

'You have my word. As you know, I'm a widower. I also never thought I'd love again. When Olivia came into my life, I realised there might be a chance. If she'll have me, and if I have your permission, I'd like to ask her to marry me.'

Keith rocked back in his seat. A smile broke across his face. From somewhere deep inside, a joyous laugh broke free. 'Really? That would be wonderful.'

The two men talked and laughed like they'd known each other for years.

'What are you two conspirators planning?' Olivia said when she returned.

'We're just exchanging notes on the special woman in our life,' Keith said. He stood and took the tray of drinks from her.

Olivia sat down beside Arthur. He took her hand.

'You have no idea how happy it makes me to see you two getting on,' Olivia said. 'I've been so apprehensive.'

Arthur raised his glass. 'I'd like to propose a toast.'

'Good idea,' Keith said.

'To friends, family and love.'

Olivia glowed. She raised her glass.

'To friends, family and love,' they all said together.

～

THE LONDON TAXI pulled up and Dicky helped Petunia out.

'Keep your eyes closed,' he said. 'No peeping.'

'What are you up to?'

'Don't look.' He held her hand and walked a short distance along the pavement to a house on the corner. He made sure she was in the right spot and then, standing behind her, said, 'You can look now.'

Petunia opened her eyes. She looked at the house, then up and down the street, then finally at Dicky. 'What? I don't understand? This is the street where I grew up.'

'Yes, it is. This house is also for sale and the agent has promised not to let anyone else view it until you and I have looked around first.'

'Really? Are you serious? You'd move back to London with me?'

'If that's what will make you happy, then that's what we'll do. I've already spoken to the company and I can get a transfer back here. They're crying out for people with my experience.'

She threw her arms around him and kissed him repeatedly. 'I love the house. It's gorgeous.'

'You haven't looked inside yet?' He dangled the keys.

She playfully grabbed them out of his hand. 'I don't need to. But since we're here, we may as well.' She ran to the front door and Dicky bounded after her.

Petunia ran excitedly from room to room. 'It's perfect. Perfect, perfect, perfect! When can we move?'

'As soon as you want to. How about straight away?'

'You really are a very special man. How did I ever get to be so lucky?'

'I have no idea,' Dicky joked.

~

'WHAT WILL YOU DO NOW?' Fleming asked. He placed his small suitcase on the back seat of his car. Next to it, wrapped in cloth, was a canvas. He'd visited Warren and bought the painting he'd seen. Try as he might, he'd been unable to shake the vision of the pensive woman from his mind.

Lily stroked Kitty, who purred in her arms. 'I'm not sure. I feel I need to get away for a while. Somewhere warm. Somewhere that isn't Fulbridge. Valerie and I had discussed Egypt to see the pyramids and journey along the Nile.'

'It would seem a fitting tribute to her,' Fleming said. 'You can certainly afford it, now you'll soon be a wealthy woman.'

'I'd give it all up in a heartbeat if it would bring back Valerie.' She sighed longingly. 'I know you insisted you didn't require payment for your services but, the truth is, I'd be spending the rest of my life behind bars if it hadn't been for you.'

'We're friends. I can't possibly take payment,' Fleming insisted.

'It's too late. I've already posted a cheque to your bank, with a note asking the manager to make sure it's credited to your account. And, one more thing, Henry Fleming, if you intend to remain my friend, you *will* accept it.'

'It that case. It's gratefully received. Thank you, Lily.' He took out his pocket watch and checked the time. 'I'd better be leaving. Inspector Carp's expecting me.'

'That man couldn't tie his shoe laces without you. I don't know how you have the patience.'

'He's young.'

'He's incompetent.'

'Perhaps. A little.'

They both chuckled.

'Where will you go after finishing with Inspector Carp today?'

'I must return to Avonbrook Cottage, Mrs Clayton's expecting me. Lewis will have finished his work. I then intend to enjoy my garden and what's left of the summer. I have books to read. Many books. Most importantly, I'll rest and not think too hard about any investigations.'

'I wish you luck with that! Though I doubt you'll be able to sit still for too long. Remember, I've known you for a very long time. It seems to me, wherever you go, trouble follows.'

Fleming pursed his lips playfully. 'That's a little unfair. Not everywhere. I once had an uneventful week in Tuscany.'

'You almost sound disappointed.'

'On the contrary. Though, as I recall, on the return trip, aboard the cruise ship, the captain was found fatally...' Fleming shook his head. 'My apologies. It appears you're right. Around every corner, a crime is lurking.'

'Whatever it is, I want you to be careful.'

He hugged Lily and gave Kitty a stroke. 'You both have my word.'

FLEMING LEANED back with his hands on his hips as he took in the view of the walled garden. He smiled with pleasure. Skip stood beside him wagging his tail.

The rose border had been weeded, fed, and mulched. The climbing roses dead-headed and tied back. The vegetable garden was regimental in appearance. The lawn mown and edged.

'Lewis, I really don't know what I'd do without you,' Fleming declared.

'It's nothing, sir. I enjoy my work.'

'It's clear to me, my enthusiasm far exceeds my abilities. If ever in the future, I suggest intruding on your domain again, I insist you bring me to my senses at once.'

'As you wish, sir.'

Skip wandered up to Lewis seeking a stroke and hopeful of a tit-bit which he duly received.

The two men, and Skip, turned at the sound of footsteps. Upon seeing Mrs Clayton's approach Lewis excused himself, leaving Fleming to talk privately to his housekeeper.

'A telegram has arrived, Mr Fleming.' She smiled at the pleasure evident on Fleming's face from seeing the garden.

'Thank you, Mrs Clayton.' He opened it and began reading. 'It's from Lily Riley.'

'I thought it might be, sir.' While Fleming read the

telegram, Mrs Clayton's eyes took in the rose garden. She was pleased the work was to Fleming's satisfaction.

'It would seem Lily has indeed decided to spread her wings. Her message informs me that she's boarded a ship to the Mediterranean. She plans to visit the historical cities of Athens and Rome. All being well, she'll then book a passage to Cairo, Egypt.'

'All thanks to you.'

'I think this calls for a celebration.'

'A celebration?'

'Yes. I think I'd enjoy a hot chocolate.'

'Of course. And where would you like to enjoy that?'

'Right here, Mrs Clayton, if you would. In the rose garden. And if you'd be so inclined, I wonder if you'd care to join me?' Fleming reached out and gently held a yellow rose. He examined it, and took in its fabulous aroma. He smiled from ear to ear. 'On a day like today, there's no place I'd rather be.'

NOTES

Henry Fleming is a man of his time who has a keen interest in all manner of new technology. It therefore seems fitting that as well as other larger vehicles he should own the new and innovative Austin 7.

The Austin 7 is an economy car that was produced from 1923 until 1939 in the United Kingdom by Austin. It was nicknamed the 'Baby Austin' and was at that time one of the most popular cars produced for the British market and sold well abroad. Its effect on the home market was similar to that of the Model T Ford in the US, replacing most other British economy cars and cyclecars of the early 1920s

Source: Wikipedia

During my research, I was surprised to learn of the rapid growth in popularity of fish and chip shops between 1910 and 1930, and the staggering fact that they first appeared in the 1860s! As soon as I learned this I simply had to include Fleming's first fish and chip supper.

Fish and chip shops first appeared in the UK in the 1860s and, by 1910, there were over 25,000 across the UK. By the 1930s there were over 35,000 shops, but the trend reversed, and by 2009 there were only approximately 10,000. The British Government safeguarded the supply of fish and chips during both the First and Second World Wars; it was one of the few foods in the UK not subject to rationing.

Source: Wikipedia

Thank you for choosing this Henry Fleming mystery. I hope you enjoyed it and will return for The Mystery of Watermead Manor.

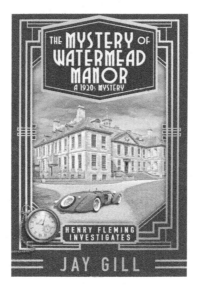

Henry Fleming Investigates
Murder in Fulbridge Village
The Mystery of Watermead Manor
Death on Damson Island
A Deadly Venetian Affair

Short Story
The Theft of the Kingsley Ruby

~

Inspector James Hardy
Chilling British Crime Thrillers

Caution: This series contains occasional strong language, moderate violence, and mild sexual references.

Knife & Death

Angels

Hard Truth

Inferno

Killing Shadows

Don't Go Home

Inspector Hardy Box Set, Books 1-3

Inspector Hardy Box Set, Books 4-6

❧

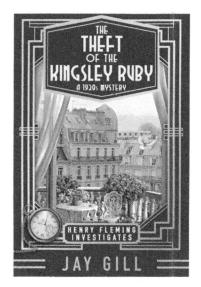

Never miss out, sign up to my mailing list and join me on Facebook, Instagram and more.

Jay Gill Newsletter
www.jaygill.net
Facebook Author Page
facebook.com/jaygillauthor
Instagram
instagram.com/jaygillauthor
Twitter
twitter.com/jaygillauthor
Bookbub
bookbub.com/authors/jay-gill
Amazon Author Page
Jay-Gill/e/B073GTM5NP

Made in the USA
Monee, IL
21 September 2022